I0551594

HUGO CHÁVEZ
THE MUSICAL!

ALVARO J. GUTIERREZ
CHAVEZMUSICAL.COM

Hugo Chávez The Musical
Published by CorpVista Media
Miami, FL

ISBN: 979-8-218-62744-7 Black and White Version
ISBN: 979-8-218-73726-9 Limited Edition Full Color

FICTION / Biographical & Autofiction
FICTION / Performing Arts / Dance, Theater & Musicals

Cover art and imagery includes AI-generated elements, arranged and finalized by the author

HUGO CHÁVEZ 1954-2013

Written as a stage script, this short novel features QR codes and hyperlinks to diverse music and dance samples. Numerous images throughout the text bring pivotal moments and key figures to life.

THIS IS A WORK OF FICTION.
Any resemblance to living persons is coincidental.

TO OPEN AUDIOVISUAL DEMOS:

Click on the links or
Scan the QR codes.

Audio and video material is
provided solely for illustrative
purposes and remains the
property of its respective owners.

CAST OF CHARACTERS
(In order of appearance)

Hugo Chávez — President of Venezuela (1999–2012)

General Velásquez — Minister of Defense

Samara — Santeria Priestess and Espiritista, longtime confidant of Hugo Chávez

Carla Garrido Bisset — American-educated journalist and TV personality, married to Marcel Grader

Jacinta — Wife of Pedro, the butler at the Garrido home

Simón Bolívar — Historical military and political leader (1783–1830), won the independence of six countries from Spain

Fidel Castro — Cuban revolutionary and dictator (1926–2016)

Pedro — Longtime butler at the Garrido home, husband to Jacinta

Olga Garrido and Martin — Carla's older sister and her husband

Doña Gabriela Garrido — Mother to the two Garrido sisters, widowed matriarch of the family

Marcel Grader — Carla Garrido's husband, head of an important media empire

Maribel — Wife of Hugo Chávez, divorced years before his death

Henderson Scooper — CNN Reporter

Nicolás Manduca — Vice President of Venezuela

Servants, soldiers, and officers. Ensemble.

ACT I
Defeat, Triumph, and the Clueless

ACT II
Power Drunk and The Curse of Simón Bolívar

Events take place over twenty years.

ACT I

SCENE 1: COUP D'ÉTAT, THE TRUE STORY

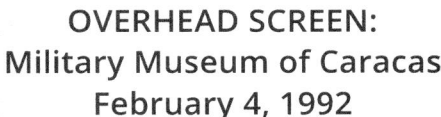

OVERHEAD SCREEN:
Military Museum of Caracas
February 4, 1992

OFFSTAGE NARRATOR: "Hugo Chávez is on the run, looking for a hiding place. The bloody coup he led has failed. Army units loyal to the government overwhelmed the rebels, who came close to assassinating the sitting president. Sporadic fighting continues in various parts of the city due to the collapse of communications between the insurgents."

AT RISE: The entire music hall darkens, and the stage goes black. "Diablos de Yare" drums erupt into a thunderous crescendo, first at a staccato pace, then faster to a furious tempo, synchronized with gunfire detonations and flashes from machine-gun muzzles.

Exhausted and battered soldiers in fatigues advance from the theater's rear through the center aisle. Pulsating strobe lights heighten the sense of danger and apprehension while they push forward, their heads turning in all directions as if stalked by nearby predators. A spotlight shows a frightened Hugo Chávez hidden in their midst. The troops encircle him protectively until they reach and climb the steps to the stage.

A burly, disheveled sergeant is in command and orders his men to stop, survey the area, and take positions. "Hide in this museum basement, Comandante. It's safe here. And stay put, because we can't risk your life—our movement depends on you. We'll come back ... if we get out of this alive."

Chávez remains silent, incapable of uttering a word as the soldiers leave him alone in the museum's underground storage.

1

He finds himself in a cramped warehouse with half-opened wood boxes containing historic war artifacts, battle paintings, and sculptures. As he walks in the dim light to inspect the storeroom, he comes across a dilapidated, large crate with oversized, stenciled "SB" letters painted red on the backside. Curious, he pries apart the loose front panel, making as little noise as possible.

What he sees amazes him.

"Oh my God! It's Simón Bolívar!" he says aloud, struggling to keep his tone down. "This must be a good omen. Maybe not all is lost."

Inside the crate is a life-size, antique, carved wood sculpture of the independence hero. Unlike the typical heroic depictions of the "Liberator" in full military regalia, this representation shows him in his early forties, dressed in casual 19th-century attire: a long coat over a vest, matching waist slash, a shirt with a blue cravat at the neck, and fitted trousers still covered with heavy wrapping paper at the lower end.

He holds an open book close to his chest with both hands while reading with a slightly inclined head. An ordinary gentleman of his era caught in a quiet, private moment, immersed in his studies.

Chávez feels compelled to touch the sculpture, like a worshipper reaching out to a venerated saint. He places his fingers on its hand, finding it unusually warm for a wooden surface.

Simón Bolívar

"Don't you feel cold in this place?" he asks, his voice low but audible to the audience. "It's freezing."

2

He rubs his arms briskly, while his gaze darts over his shoulder, fearing someone might be following him.

"What are you studying, Bolívar? The story of the rebellion I led—the uprising now crumbling around us? Is it already written?"

He stoops, attempting to read the book title, but can only discern a few blurred letters: *DR FAUS*. The others are illegible.

He stares at Bolívar.

"I know what you're thinking. I'm hiding in this museum while young conscripts die fighting in my name. But if I survive, I will make it up to you, our great Liberator, and devote my life to bettering the lot of our people, just as you did. I promise!"

Chávez sings in the evocative style of the Adagio from "Concierto de Aranjuez."

Bolívar Is My Witness

The truth hides
With me in this basement.
I deserted my comrades,
While they continue to fight.
Yet Bolívar is here, beside me still,
He knows, understands
Though I may fall, though I may flee,
A higher purpose is my destiny.
Bolívar is my witness.
He stands with me today.

During the song, a ray of light pierces the prevailing darkness, illuminating the wood Liberator inside the crate. The statue lifts its head toward Chávez almost imperceptibly, seemingly straining to catch the words.

Chávez cuts short his singing at the sound of noises and agitated voices nearby. Before he can run, two SWAT members rappel from above on ropes within feet of him. He panics as the side doors of the storage room burst apart with a controlled explosion. Gunfire echoes and strobe lights deluge the stage.

More men rush in to apprehend the leader of the rebellion, cursing and pointing their Glocks at him in double-handed firing positions.

"Here's the son of a whore! ¡Aquí está el hijo de puta!" says a soldier.

"Is that him?" asks another. "Hiding like a scared girl? While his companions die in the streets defending him?"

With a look of terror on his face, Chávez raises his arms as the soldiers close in on him. They shout furious insults, rough him up, and force him to kneel with his hands behind his back. The captain of the team points a gun at his head.

Chávez starts to sob and tremble. "Please don't kill me. Please, please, please. I can explain everything."

"You cowardly dog! I should blow your brains out right now," the officer says, jabbing him with his pistol.

As this occurs, the statue of Bolívar follows along in slow motion, shifting side to side. Amid the uproar, nobody notices the shadowy figure concealed by the surrounding boxes.

A loud voice from the rear interrupts the scuffle. "Stop it, you idiots! Help him up. We need to find out who else is involved in this conspiracy."

"Yes, sir, General Velásquez," the captain says, turning to his subordinates. "Move it! Didn't you hear the Minister of Defense?"

Muttering their disapproval, the soldiers release their grip on the insurrectionist, who is still in shock when he confronts the general, a tall man with a pronounced mustache.

The two stare at each other as if they have met before. Gen. Velásquez edges nearer to the coup's leader and whispers something quickly in his ear, unobserved by the others.

The prisoner gives a faint nod and says, "OK."

Velásquez then spins around, asks for a couple of chairs and a table, and sits down, inviting Chávez to do the same with a courteous motion of his hand. A brief private negotiation ensues.

Meanwhile, the rest of the men loitering about form a vocal combo. Mocking facial expressions and gestures match the singing in the manner of "Serenata Guayanesa."

Just Shoot the Bastard

What are those two negotiating?
Take the bastard outside already.
Line him up against a nice wall,
And shoot him.
What are we waiting for?
Shoot the bastard.
Line him up against a nice wall.
Shoot, shoot, shoot.

The general and Chávez continue their conversation off to the side, a wordless and muffled dialogue that sounds at a distance like "hum-hum, hum-hum, hum-hum."

Gen. Velásquez rises, shakes Chávez's hand vigorously, and announces in a booming voice, "We will allow the Lieutenant Colonel to address his troops on national television and order them to surrender to avoid further bloodshed. Clear the way!"

A swarm of journalists and TV crews with camcorders and boom mikes storm the room and besiege the unknown army colonel. Straightening his uniform, he retrieves his signature red beret from the floor and puts it on. Behind him, a group of officers joins Gen. Velásquez, all vying for prime spots before such an important broadcast. The Simón Bolívar sculpture, concealed in its crate, seems to stir—its head tilting toward the speaker.

February 4, 1992

5

Staring at the cameras, microphones all around him, Chávez starts his "Por Ahora" (for the time being) one-minute speech, the most memorable in his lifetime. He sings, emulating "I Will Survive."

For the Time Being

Comrades in arms.
Listen to me, Comandante Chávez.
We did not achieve our goals,
For the time being.

This introduction breaks into a rhythmic, danceable part. Chávez moves with the music while remaining at the center of the group.

Lay down your arms.
No more bloodshed for our noble cause.
Stand proud for your bravery, your loyalty, your sacrifice.
We will survive to see a brighter future.

All journalists and officers are now swaying in unison, even as they surround the speaker, who continues singing.

Our people deserve a better fate,
Let us reflect on this sad state.
The blame is mine. I bear it all,
Before the world, I take the fall.
Surrender your weapons,
But never your spirit.
We will survive, comrades.

A spotlight shines on a tall, attractive twenty-eight-year-old who is up front among the pack of reporters. She sways to the rhythm, while keeping a small recorder in her extended arm close to the defeated colonel.

The action freezes.

OFFSTAGE NARRATOR: "This is Carla Garrido Bisset, a well-known journalist, writer, and popular television host. A Princeton graduate, she comes from a prominent, high-society family."

The action resumes.

Following his brief speech, Chávez notices Carla in the crowd, drawn by her slender figure and long, dark hair. They exchange looks in silence for a few seconds before guards lead him away.

As she leaves with the rest of the press, a colleague says, "What balls! … Um, sorry for my language, but I am mad as hell."

"Why? What made you so angry?"

"He says they didn't accomplish their objectives 'for the time being.' Just getting started? Is that it?"

"He is audacious, I have to admit."

"I hope they lock him up for life. We haven't had a coup in this country for decades."

"All I can tell you is that I'm impressed," she says. "What composure! And he is very brave. I mean, his captors could have killed him minutes earlier. But he seemed in full control. And millions are watching on TV."

The two exit together.

Unnoticed during the media frenzy, Simón Bolívar's wooden statue silently shuts the book and lowers it to its side. It walks to the rear with slow and measured steps, pauses at the end of Chávez's speech, nods in agreement, and then escapes.

A crate with "SB" written on it remains behind—empty.

FADEOUT

SCENE 2: SAMARA'S VISION IN PRISON

OVERHEAD SCREEN:
A Military Prison
March 1994

OFFSTAGE NARRATOR: "The government has held Chávez in custody for over two years. He receives a constant and ever-growing stream of admirers in his comfortable quarters."

SETTING: Chávez's private suite, a sanctuary within the prison walls, resembles a threadbare but ample apartment. It contains a refrigerator, TV set, hanging cocoon hammock near a wall, and other essential furniture. The adjacent reception area, visible to the audience, shows a diverse crowd of ordinary folks, fans, friends, and well-known personalities from the political, business, and media elites.

AT RISE: The stage is a beehive of activity. A group of politicians in coats and ties, off in a corner, engage in an animated conversation. In the middle are clusters of humble people, young and old—some sitting, others standing—bringing fruits and homemade dishes for el Comandante. An elderly woman with a faded headscarf, wearing her kitchen apron, holds a live chicken in a cage, a gift for Chávez. Awaiting their turn with the now-famous prisoner are journalists with ID tags hanging around their necks and businessmen clutching briefcases and papers. The air is thick with anticipation and nervous energy, visitors unsure of what to expect from the popular rebel leader.

A stranger arrives and immediately becomes the center of attention.

As she strides imperiously into the large, packed room, all eyes are on her. Several men rise out of respect and offer her a seat. Her exotic, spotless white robe, flowing to her feet, captivates the women, as do the visitor's chain necklaces and tribal collar. Gold bracelets form undulating tubes on her forearms down to her wrists. Most striking is the red embroidered emblem on her traditional head wrap, a symbol of her elevated rank as an Olorisha Santera. The awe and reverence she inspires are palpable, leaving everyone hushed and motionless in her presence.

9

Remarkably attractive and slender at forty, with a beautiful face and a raw sensuality to her movements, the imposing, over six-foot-tall black woman from Barlovento steals the limelight wherever she goes.

"That's Samara," says the sergeant stationed at the entrance to Chávez's quarters to a guard who is new to the post. "She often comes to visit."

The young man, visibly nervous, says, "I can't believe she is standing in front of us."

"That's her," the veteran says, while getting closer to the rookie and adopting a more confidential tone, "the famous Santeria priestess known for her supernatural powers and prophecies."

Samara from Barlovento, a region with a predominantly Black population from colonial times.

He lowers his voice. "And let me tell you, she's consulted by the rich and powerful of this country, including presidents."

Impressed, the youthful sentry stays riveted to the floor, his gaze fixed on the revered visionary.

"Move it! What are you waiting for? Go over and pay your respects," the officer says.

The junior guard approaches the guest. "Pardon me, Señora Samara," he asks, "could you please wait a minute while I inform el Comandante you've arrived? He'll be happy to see you."

When he enters to announce the priestess, the prisoner sits at a table reading papers.

As Samara steps in, Chávez greets her with a hug and a friendly peck on the cheek, rising on his toes because she is much taller than him.

10

"Hope you have something great to tell me today, Samara. I'm not in the mood for gloomy predictions."

"Good and bad, Hugo. Up to you which way things go, now that you're so popular. And I will help you, but only if you trust and listen to me."

"Of course I trust you. Always have, ever since I was a cadet. But you scare the hell out of me sometimes. Who else knows the past, present, and future as well as you do?"

"I am on your side, don't forget. But so far, all I envision is a dense fog. When it disperses, I want to be certain that the sun shines bright and clear."

She turns away from Chávez and spots Simón Bolívar's wood figure in a corner. Surprised, she asks, "What's that doing there?" pointing at it.

"You won't believe this. Remember what I told you about those terrible hours I spent at the military museum during the coup? Totally isolated in the basement, not knowing the fate of my comrades or whether I would live or die."

"Yes, I remember that story. Also, the unkind comments about a commanding officer hiding while his men were still under fire. Wasn't your finest hour, Hugo."

"I had no choice! Government troops outnumbered us and we were pinned down under heavy gunfire. That was the nearest building where we could find cover."

He becomes agitated, pacing back and forth in the room.

"I wanted to keep fighting, Samara—believe me! But the sergeant in charge of our unit refused to let me go. Didn't want to risk losing the leader of our movement, he said."

"I thought *you* were in charge, Hugo. But never mind, let's forget it. Just tell me what all of this has to do with the statue of Bolívar."

"It was a present from some of my classmates at the Academy. They brought it along when they visited me. But that's not the incredible part."

"What is? Plenty of images of the Liberator in military installations. It's not surprising that they would give you one."

"Here is the thing. The day before they came over, guards found that statue abandoned in the parking lot of the army base. Nobody had any idea how or when someone had placed it there."

"That's odd …"

"When Captain Arias, the organizer of the group, saw the sculpture, he thought it would make a great gift since he knows how much I admire El Libertador. So they loaded it on a truck to bring it here."

"All right, the story is unusual. But what's the big mystery?"

"Wait until you hear the rest! The whole incident is out of this world, I swear, because I had seen and touched that very same statue before. And you know where? In the museum's basement the day of my detention. Simón Bolívar was with me at the most difficult moment of my life."

"Oh really? And how did you happen to bump into him there? Did the two of you shake hands?"

"No, no. I stumbled upon a large old crate, and the sight of "SB" marked outside in big, red letters made me curious. So, I looked inside, and that's when I first saw the sculpture."

"Are you sure it is the same?"

"Yes! It resembled a real person in the dim light, very different from the typical carvings of our independence hero."

She walks over to the figure. "You're right. Never seen anything like it. Very casual, as if relaxing at home, strolling immersed in a book."

"¡Correcto! What's he reading? What's he thinking? Know what I mean?"

"Nothing remains hidden from the Spirits, Hugo. They understand the reason for your encounter that night and will explain it to me."

"Whatever they say is going to be absolutely fabulous! I'm convinced of that."

"I hope so."

12

"Anyway, I've gotten used to Bolívar being around. It gets lonely after everybody leaves. I even talk to him after dark."

"Do you?"

"Yep. And guess what? He pays attention. He looks at me as if he understands."

"How long have you had these thoughts, Hugo?"

While this conversation is underway, figures in the adjoining waiting area, silhouetted behind a translucent screen, move in silence, as if suspended in time.

"Let's be serious, if you don't mind," she says. "Hear me out. It's important."

She sings in a deep, passionate voice in the style of "Nessun Dorma" by Puccini, while Chávez listens attentively:

My Vision of You, Hugo

My words are timeless, Hugo
Pathways to the future,
Anchored to the past.

I see you leading our people
To the Promised Land,
Where chains are broken,
From the slavery of poverty.
I see you sheltering the weak
The children, the elderly, the hungry.

Hugo, Hugo, never betray us!
Do not let power cloud your mind.
Do not allow riches to spoil you.

When you reach the mountaintop,
Remember, you come from humble stock.
Should you forget who you are,
Unimaginable suffering
Will claim your life and soul.

While the song plays on, visitors from next door trickle in unnoticed. Couples come into view, dancing a folkloric joropo with a muted accompaniment, pirouetting with its typical footwork.

Samara and Chávez are so engrossed in the aria that they are startled when the dancers encircling them burst into a joyful chorus and dance:

Chávez Is Our Savior

Chávez, Chávez, Chávez, sí!
Our savior, strong and brave.
Come to help and lift the poor,
A voice of hope for our people
He is one of us, a humble man.
Chávez, Chávez, Chávez, sí!

Chávez, an accomplished joropo singer and dancer, joins the festivities, whirling and stomping his feet, hands behind his back with the rest of the crowd. Just then, Carla Garrido Bisset, the journalist, shows up for her meeting with the Comandante, suitably dressed for the rough prison setting in pants and a jeans jacket.

A reporter nearby comes over and asks—amid the dancing and singing—"Carla, what are you doing here? Never expected to run into you in this place."

"I came to interview the Lieutenant Colonel, like the rest of the press."

"With your influence, I bet you got an appointment real quick. Me? I've been waiting for days. Anyway, what do you think? All these people seem to adore Chávez. Look at them."

She nods in agreement as the gathering disperses. "Amazing how el pueblo loves this man. You can feel it in the air."

The dancers and the news reporter exit.

When Samara bids Chávez farewell, he leans in and says, "I need you here often. Your guidance shines a light on the future."

The guards escort her out as befits someone of importance, looking dignified, keeping their distance behind her with their heads tilted upward.

Carla remains in the room.

14

SCENE 3: CARLA AND CHÁVEZ ALONE

When Chávez notices Carla, he hastens toward her.

"Carla Garrido Bisset. How good to meet you," he says as he shakes her hand with both of his. "I am honored that such a famous journalist and TV personality would take the trouble to visit me in this dump. And such a beautiful and intelligent woman." He smiles as he scrutinizes her from top to bottom.

"Colonel, many others are still waiting for you. So I suggest we start the interview, because I have lots of questions."

"OK. I'm ready." They sit across a table in the room.

"By the way, I couldn't help noticing how much warmth you showed the group that just left."

"Whatever bond I have with my people, mi pueblo, is heartfelt. That's why they come and believe in me."

"I know, I know. Millions outside these prison walls share the same feelings after seeing you on TV the night of the coup. I was there as a member of the press. Heard your 'for the time being' speech, which is now famous."

"Doesn't take a journalist to understand why common folk admire me. I am one of them. It's that simple. I'm from humble origins, not to mention my lowly appearance. Nobody would mistake me for a Garrido Bisset, don't you think?"

Carla meets Chávez in prison 1994

15

Carla laughs. "Well, for whatever reasons, your popularity grows daily, even while imprisoned. You have a great political career ahead of you, and I am interested in your plans when you get out of this 'dump,' as you call it."

"Shoot," he replies.

"What do you intend to do?"

"Tell the truth."

"That's marvelous. But could you be a little more specific?"

As this conversation unfolds, the adjacent waiting room, dimmed after the departure of the joropo dancers, lights up behind a translucent partition. A group of unkempt street urchins in tattered and filthy clothing enters from the rear. Some find a spot on the floor, while others remain standing.

"Want to know what's wrong in this country, do you? Look at them," he says, his voice tinged with resentment as he points to the see-through screen. "What do you think these kids are doing, Carla? They are scavenging for food in piles of garbage."

"Yes, it's tragic. It breaks my heart, especially the younger, defenseless little ones with nowhere to go."

Chávez promised to resign if he did not solve the problem of "niños de la calle." Thousands still roam the streets searching for food in garbage piles.

"I've seen the faces of homeless children roaming our cities, their eyes filled with hunger and despair," Chávez says with indignation.

Carla directs her gaze toward the room-size living tableau and says,

16

"Over there, I make out two boys and a small girl on the sidewalk, eating leftovers from a torn trash bag. And a couple of older kids by a dumpster eating garbage."

"Why is this happening in our country?" she asks, as the lights fade out behind the partition.

"And what about the millions in those miserable slums, Carla? Barrios surrounding our cities, cordons of misery, crime, and drugs amid the vast wealth of the privileged classes."

His voice grows louder and more passionate as he expresses his bitterness. He stands abruptly, knocking over a glass of water, and clutches the back of his chair, his head lowered, with anger on his face. "Does anyone care about our poor? Nobody gives a damn!"

They lock eyes in a tense staring contest, her unwavering gaze meeting his. "I agree," she says after a pause. "Poverty is a ticking time bomb. We must act before it is too late."

"Yes, because we won't take it anymore."

Chávez sings an eloquent bolero while standing. As he gets more emotional and the tempo picks up, he moves around the stage in rhythm with the music.

Our People Won't Take It Anymore

Forty years of darkness, injustice, and neglect,
While they disdain our struggle, our loss, their gain.
We won't take it anymore, no more!

Why should we drown in filth?
While the rich laugh and click glasses on their yachts.
We won't take it anymore!

Oh no, not again, not today, not tomorrow—
Our people must rise, no more begging or sorrow.
We won't take it anymore!

17

Toward the end of his singing, he approaches Carla and tries pulling her to her feet to dance the bolero. She declines and remains seated. The song ends as he sees Jacinta entering the room carrying his meal tray.

She is a chubby, not unattractive, dark-skinned fortyish woman with pronounced hips and a generous rump, who Chávez greets warmly.

"Hola, Jacinta! Thanks for bringing my lunch. Just set it down for me, and I'll eat it later."

"Carla, this wonderful lady is one of the few good things that has happened to me while locked up here. The warden hired her to cook for me, but she helps with everything these days. Looks after me like a mama bear over her cub."

"Oh yes, I am well acquainted with Jacinta and her husband, Pedro."

"Small world! Where did you meet them?"

"Pedro has been at my mother's house for ages."

"Comandante, Señora Carla means to say that my husband has been the butler at her family's mansion for the past twenty years. I've dropped him off there many times."

She puts down her tray at the table.

"I am surprised to find you here, Señora Carla. When I tell Pedro you visited el Comandante, he will be pleased. But your mother won't be too happy if she finds out. I suspect that Doña Gabriela and her friends are no fans of Señor Chávez."

"It's part of my job, Jacinta. But I'm glad to see you too. Been a while since you've come to my mother's house."

"My hands are full cooking and caring for this very special prisoner. I rarely have time for anything else. But it is the most important thing in my life."

"I can imagine it. Pedro mentioned that both of you are great admirers of the Colonel."

"Yes, we are." She looks at Chávez, who is paying close attention to the conversation between the women. "We'll do whatever it takes to help him lead us to a better future."

18

"I don't doubt it. Many others also support him."

"We do not have much schooling, as you know. But like everybody in the barrios, we are sure el Comandante is destined for greatness."

"This is embarrassing me," Chávez says. "You ladies are too serious. Carla refuses to dance with me. But you love salsa. C'mon Jacinta!"

He grabs her hand and draws her toward him for a lively merengue while the journalist looks on with amusement from her seat.

Laughing and smiling, Jacinta matches Chávez's movements in step with the captivating tropical beat. "Comandante!" she says whenever he pulls and turns her vigorously.

A classic from the late '60s, "Apágame la Vela María," has suggestive lyrics about "blowing out my burning candle, María."

As the two continue dancing in the background with the music muted, Carla goes off to the side and sings in the style of a romantic ballad:

He Says all the Right Things

Does he care for the poor?
Or is it just a ploy,
A clever disguise
To chase power and fame?
Can I trust him?
My heart whispers, yes.
But my mind, says no.
I've seen this before.
His words are so smooth,
He says all the right things,
But I've heard them before.
Is he different, or just like the rest?
I want to believe,
But I can't shake off the distrust.

19

When the pair ends their dance, Carla stops singing and sees Jacinta walking toward the exit, who says, "Señora Carla, you are in safe hands with el Comandante," as she winks with a slight smile.

The journalist and Chávez are finally alone. He comes near her, now back in her seat.

"And how do you propose eradicating all that misery, Colonel? Another coup? More death and destruction?"

"Oh, no! This time, it's going to be peaceful and democratic. I plan to leave it to clever people like you to figure out how and when to run for president. And win."

He then swivels and thrusts his face closer, intensity palpable in his voice.

"Will you help me? Your audience is huge, and your husband controls RVTV, a media empire. You both know the rich and powerful of this country."

He pauses, edges nearer, and continues with greater fervor.

"With your backing, we have a shot at the presidency, to make it to Miraflores. Can I count on you?"

He places his hand on hers on the table. She pulls her arm away and replies, "You have charisma, but you think and act like a leftist populist. That is always seductive to the masses. But, keeping your promises requires more than beautiful speeches."

Miraflores, historic seat of government in Caracas.

She confronts Chávez eye to eye. "Aren't you driven by personal gain and ambition? How do I know? I've seen power corrupt even the most well-intentioned leaders."

"Those with eyes shall see. Those with ears shall hear."

20

"You use that biblical phrase often, don't you? What you see is what you get. Is that what you're saying?"

"¡Sí! The truth is in plain view. I told you that at the beginning."

"If and when the government releases you, how will you persuade an entire nation that the leader of a bloody coup is worthy of getting elected? That's impossible."

"I am going to prove you wrong. Mark my words."

"I doubt it, because I've read some of your other interviews. Troubling, to say the least. Your raw ambition and thirst for power come through."

"You've done your research. But judge me by my future actions, not by articles written about me."

"True. But you have already revealed much about yourself. Autocratic tendencies and questionable morals. Ingredients for loss of freedom and corruption should you become president someday."

"You are very harsh on me. But you will change your mind. Just give me a chance to—"

She interrupts him.

"As of today, Colonel, I'm not convinced. I've seen and heard enough. Good day."

She exits, leaving Chávez alone in his large prison room.

SCENE 4: SOLEMN PACT WITH SIMÓN BOLÍVAR

Chávez, now by himself, teases the wood sculpture. "What do you think, little Simón? ¿Qué piensas, Simoncito?"

He strides to the statue, playfully pats it on the cheek, and hangs his red beret on its top. "Can I win the support of the powerful oligarchs? Of the shit that fertilizes only their own crop? While the rest of us starve."

He returns to the table, disregards the food that Jacinta had brought for him, and flops into a chair, sighing with exhaustion. He holds his head with his palm, elbow resting on the tabletop, and seems to doze off.

The sculpture becomes animated and walks to the sitting prisoner.

"Chávez!" Bolívar says in a commanding voice while shaking him awake.

Startled out of his slumber, he turns to face Simón Bolívar. Incredulous, he jumps to his feet, comes to attention, and raises his hand to his forehead to give the Liberator a crisp army salute.

"Mi General. What are *you* doing here?"

"That is not thy concern."

The insurrectionist officer remains ramrod straight, arms locked at his sides.

"Thy conduct at the military museum was dishonorable, a total disgrace. 'Twas cowardly for a commander to hide and abandon his men amid battle."

Chávez clenches his fists, holds his breath, and does not dare make a sound.

"Yet thou art the lesser of two evils. I could wait another century until a proper leader comes forth, or support thee, despite my grave doubts about thy valor."

The Liberator draws closer.

"I sacrificed and risked too much, labored too diligently to liberate this land of

23

plenty, only to witness it descend into corruption, inequality, and injustice. 'Tis time to take action."

He starts to sing. Chávez soon joins him in a duet in the style of a "Perfect Symphony."

A Beautiful Revolution

Bolívar:
We need a revolution,
Not one of blood or war, no, no,
But a beautiful revolution,
A peaceful wave to even the score,
To lift the poor from suffering at last,
And heal the wounds of ages past.

Chávez:
I believe it too, mi General,
With every beat, with every breath.
It's what I dream, what I fight for,
What I'll live for 'til my death.
A beautiful revolution.

Bolívar & Chávez:
We need a revolution,
Not violent, as in times before, no, no,
A beautiful revolution,
A peaceful call to change the world once more.

Bolívar waves impatiently at the orchestra and orders it to stop. "Silence!"

"Let us to our work," he says. "Though I harbor doubts, I plan to offer thee an opportunity to achieve great deeds for this country or slide into oblivion like most men. But you must first sign and honor a solemn pact. You shalt fulfill thy part, and I mine."

"Yes, sir!"

"I will arrange to get thee out of here, guide thy path to the presidency, and command Samara to keep an eye on thee. Heed her counsel, for she knows the afterlife."

"Where do I put my signature?" Chávez asks, rubbing his hands like a hungry man invited to a feast.

"Not so hasty."

Bolívar pulls out of his pocket a rolled-up scroll with a tricolor ribbon—yellow, blue, and red. Tucked inside is a quill feather pen. He unfolds the parchment, lays it flat on the table, and points to it.

"Sign here. Affirm before God and me that thou wilt honor this oath to lead a beautiful revolution and transform this land for all time."

Hesitating for a moment, Chávez picks up the manuscript with shaky hands, aware of the seriousness of the obligation he is about to assume. He reads, signs, and recites it:

> "I, Hugo Chávez, do solemnly swear before the Almighty and you, our Liberator, to lead a beautiful revolution and to tirelessly defend, protect, and improve the lives of our people. My power, be it great or small, shall ever remain at the service of my country. I shall brook no corruption, for honesty and integrity shall be my guiding stars. I vow to uphold this sacred pledge until my dying breath. So help me, God."

"God shall not help thee, Chávez, if you dare break this pact between us. I have shot many a traitor in my days, yet if you forsake the people, neglect the impoverished, and descend into the depths of dishonesty, a fate far worse than that of a defector awaits thee."

Chávez stands motionless, his eyes widening in fear of Bolívar's words as sweat drips down his face.

"Never forget that! Thou shalt beg for the firing squad, so agonizing shall be thy death should thou betrayest me and our cause."

Bolívar glances at his pocket watch as if short on time, picks up the parchment, and strides off, a lone spotlight trailing behind him as the stage darkens.

FADE OUT

SCENE 5: LAST TANGO IN LA HABANA

OVERHEAD SCREEN:
Fidel Castro's Home
June 1994

OFFSTAGE NARRATOR: "The government unexpectedly releases Chávez, who makes his first trip abroad to Cuba at the personal invitation of Fidel Castro. After the public events, the two meet privately in the Cuban dictator's den in his residence. So intimate is this informal hideout that Castro sentenced a staff member who dared enter without permission to five years of hard labor."

SETTING: The room's decoration is a mismatch of valuable gifts from heads of state mixed with odds and ends, including a spattering of plastic plants. Rustic, turquoise-blue plank walls recreate the ones in Castro's humble childhood home. Little Fidel and his siblings, illegitimate children of their father and his mistress—a former house cook—lived in a small cottage on the elder Castro's farm, quite a distance from the principal residence.

Slightly separated from the main sitting area, there is a smaller connected room lined with framed pictures on the walls. Curiously, most of these black-and-white photos from the 1960s depict shirtless young men, some in casual, suggestive poses, others flexing their muscles.

AT RISE: Castro drinks Cuba Libre vodka, custom-made for him at a Siberian prison camp, while Chávez has a glass of Cuatro Gatos rum, the cheapest on the island. The host sits in his favorite brown leatherette armchair, and his guest is on the large matching sofa.

Chávez can barely contain himself when he says, "Comandante, I am still in shock by the honor of being welcomed by you personally on the runway when I stepped off the plane."

"Don't mention it. You deserve that and more." Castro gestures with his hand to dismiss the matter.

27

"I won't forget it till I die! As I walked down the steps and caught sight of you, I couldn't believe my eyes. Was that really Fidel, I thought, or another tall, handsome guy in fatigues, perhaps a guard?"

"Hugo, you are a courageous officer who just got out of prison after leading a dangerous coup that came close to succeeding. You are my type of man. That's why I invited you and will greet you myself any day, con gusto."

Chávez fidgets nervously with his glass, awestruck by the legendary figure before him. Castro's magnetic presence, almost erotic in its intensity up close, strongly attracts Chávez. Could it be, he wonders, that their first private meeting might blossom into something more intimate?

"Anyway," Castro says, jolting Chávez from his reverie, "we have much to discuss. You are young, talented, and crave power above all else, as you have told me so many times. Well, I have useful advice for you."

"I am all ears, Comandante. Not everyone has the privilege of being guided by a leader admired by millions."

"Tomorrow, we'll get into more complicated matters, but for this afternoon, I advise you to do three simple things."

"And what are those?"

"First, keep your communist beliefs hidden. Once you are in charge, let them out slowly, like toothpaste from a tube, little by little every morning."

The new pupil nods in agreement.

"Second, always pretend to be a socialist. That's your ticket to respectability. Sure, it scares the hell out of your middle class, but Europeans lap it up. They love the socialist bullshit and think it is the magic cure for all the problems of poor countries."

He pauses, letting his words sink in before resuming.

"And intellectuals? García Márquez, Noam Chomsky, and their like? Man, they will kiss your ass as long as you act like a leftist progressive."

"And what about the gringos? How should I deal with them?"

"It's easy. All they care about is business. So, always remember to mention the private sector is crucial for the country's development. That keeps them happy."

He gets up, walks over to the side table in the adjoining room, and pours another drink for both of them before returning to his seat.

"One last thing. Get yourself a beautiful trophy wife ASAP. Latinos are macho societies, regardless of the women's liberation crap. Humble folk love to see their caudillo in the company of stunning women."

Chávez pays close attention.

"A few illegitimate kids here and there, you know, as I have, also makes a great impression. Looks terrific."

The master's words hold the listener captive.

"That's your lesson for the day. Take note because it will come in handy soon." As he says this, he reaches toward the couch and places his hand on Chávez's.

The visitor does not move it away as the two men stare at each other.

"My, what a delicate hand, Hugo, soft as a girl's. Did anybody ever tell you that?" He strokes it gently.

Chávez remains quiet, with his eyes fixed on Fidel, who stands, then sits beside him, forcing him to slide over. They wind up so tight on the sofa that they can feel each other's warmth.

Chávez freezes as if under a spell when Fidel lays his palm on his knee. With his broad and corpulent frame, the Cuban strongman overwhelms the smaller man as he leans over.

No longer upright, Chávez eases into a reclining position while Castro moves his fingers toward the inner thigh of his now willing guest. He fondles Chávez, mounts him, and kisses him on the neck, then on the mouth.

Aroused, Chávez breathes heavily, parts his legs, and starts rotating his hips to match Castro's rhythmic thrusts. Chávez adjusts his posture, fumbling with his belt to lower his trousers. But suddenly, Castro interrupts the intimacy, rising to plant an affectionate kiss on Chávez's forehead.

"Later, Hugo. Let's wait till later. Tonight, we'll be alone again." He sits up and gets to his feet.

Chávez hesitates, lingering on the couch before standing and straightening out his rumpled pants and coat. While facing each other, Castro caresses Chávez's face. "You are going to confront many obstacles to attain power. But I promise to protect you. I'm your man."

Chávez nestles against Castro's chest and embraces him. His eyes water and his voice quivers with emotion. "I don't know if I have the strength to lead a country without you, Fidel. I need you by my side."

Castro pushes him away, wrinkling his nose at the smell of Chávez's hair. "Let's talk about that tomorrow," he says. "For now, let me give you a surprise."

"What more surprise than what just happened?"

"I want you to dance with me. I hear you are an excellent dancer, and I am pretty good at the tango. Che Guevara taught me decades ago. Gorgeous man, that Che."

He leads his guest to the next room, which Chávez had not yet seen.

After gazing at the framed pictures on the walls, Chávez says, "Comandante! What a beautiful collection of photographs."

"Thanks. I thought you would like them. They were the last gift el Che gave me before he was killed in Bolivia."

Castro then walks over to the expensive stereo to load and play a CD of a popular, syncopated tango.

He steps in front of Chávez and wraps his arm around him, embracing him tightly, while their hands clasp together at shoulder level.

"Comandante, I know nothing about tangos!"

"Don't worry. This is all macho. I lead, and you follow obediently. Today, you're my woman."

A perfectly executed tango, in the style of "La Cumparsita," ensues between the pair.

The footwork is elaborate, precise, and elegant, of the more intimate and subdued variety.

After Chávez departs, Castro says under his breath, "Who knows? Given time—and a little meddling on our part—we might just get this fool elected president. And then, oh my … all that oil money will keep us afloat forever."

An intimate tango in Castro's den.

He walks to his desk, opens a drawer, and turns off the concealed recorder and cameras.

FADE OUT

SCENE 6: THE ENEMY WITHIN

OVERHEAD SCREEN:
Garrido Bisset Mansion
December 1997

OFFSTAGE NARRATOR: "Doña Gabriela, the widowed matriarch of the Garrido family, is having dinner at her home in the city's wealthiest neighborhood with her two daughters, Olga, the eldest, and Carla, together with their husbands."

SETTING: As is the rest of the mansion, the elegant dining room is decorated in a sober, Spanish Colonial style, with a solid bronze ceiling chandelier dominating the space. An antique Persian tapestry complements numerous lithographs on the walls. Massive, hand-carved wooden doors open onto an internal patio, accommodating larger gatherings when required.

A partition divides the stage, revealing an old-fashioned kitchen in the other half when illuminated. As the scene shifts back to the dining room, the kitchen area darkens.

AT RISE: Pedro, the slender, Black house butler in a white jacket and gloves, serves the guests around the table.

Pedro, butler at the Garrido Bisset home.

Martin, Olga's husband, is complaining about his upcoming vacation. "I have been trying to reach Monsieur Dubois in Courchevel, and that idiot won't even return my calls or answer my faxes. Did he forget how often my family has stayed at his ski resort in the Alps?"

33

"What do you expect?" says his wife. "Courchevel has become the latest status symbol for Caracas' new money. Everyone is going there. No wonder you can't get reservations."

"Maybe so," Doña Gabriela says, as she dabs her lips with the linen napkin, "but just to be safe, why don't you go to Vail instead? They tell me it's also very nice."

"Yes, Mother," Olga says. "We are considering Colorado or something more affordable. Europe is out of control."

"I am glad for you. What a relief!"

"Skiing is becoming too expensive," Martin says, "besides putting up with all those low-class, filthy rich people. They are taking over our hotels and resorts. Money talks, you see."

"Carla, what do you think?" asks her older sister, sitting across from her, near the aristocratic matriarch of the family. "Your opinion has always been the most important around here ever since you went to Princeton. You're the smart one, aren't you?"

"We're at risk of losing our winter holidays," she replies in a serious tone, pretending to deliver terrible news. Next to her is Marcel Grader, her husband, owner of a prominent media empire.

"You are right, Olga," he says. "It takes Carla's degree to explain what ails this country: The end of ski vacations as we know them. Heaven forbid!"

The guests sing a humorous chorus lamenting this disaster, interspersed by short solos. Each person has a brief role that merges with the rest of the ensemble.

The End of Ski Vacations as We Know Them

Martin:	*My skiing vacation will cost me a fortune this year.*
Olga:	*What is happening to prices in Courchevel?*
Doña Gabriela:	*Stay calm, my darlings, we have survived worse things.*
Carla:	*A crisis of historic proportions is upon us!*

Olga: *Our human rights are being trampled.*
Marcel: *It's The End of Ski Vacations as We Know Them.*
All: *Oh no, oh dear, how could this be?*
The gondola fees? Simply out of this world!
No foie gras at the lodge? We're losing it all!
The end of ski vacations is here to stay!

Meanwhile, the butler leaves the dining room, walking past a swinging door on his way back to the large kitchen visible onstage. There, a rotund male cook, Remberto, and a couple of maids, Salvadora and Juana, work feverishly, preparing the rest of the meal.

Pedro enters and addresses the staff. "We ain't going to Courchevel this year, folks."

All turn toward him with curiosity on their faces.

"Too many low-class people and too damn expensive. But no problem. I got a better idea."

"So, where are we vacationing this season?" asks Salvadora. "Don't keep us in suspense."

"Have you ever been to Vail? No? I thought so. How about you two?"

"Nope," replies the cook.

"Well … it was a long time ago," says Juana. "I was just a baby. Don't remember much."

Pedro sings, joined by the others. They satirize the hardships facing them with biting sarcasm. The men complain about the expense, the maids about having to discard outdated attires. Latino rhythms accompany the four voices:

We Ain't Going to Courchevel, No Sir!

Men: *Where are we going skiing this year?*
Courchevel too expensive, oh dear!
Crowded with filthy rich, low-class folk.

We ain't going to Courchevel, no joke!
Second-rate Vail is now our hope.

Women: *We have to toss out all our clothes,*
Ski outfits looking tired, heaven knows!
Last season's jackets, so old-fashioned.

Men and Women: *Where are we going skiing this year?*
We ain't going to Courchevel, that's clear.

As the singing wanes, the guests at the table engage in a loud political discussion. They argue about the presidential aspirations of Hugo Chávez, the military leader of the failed 1992 coup—five years earlier—that almost toppled the government.

Martin, having downed a few too many drinks, anger showing in his face, says, "That son of a bitch is a murderer. Please excuse my language, Doña Gabriela, but I don't understand why they pardoned him. A life sentence is what he deserves!"

"Outrageous!" Olga says, "A mestizo and a communist. Can you imagine him as our president?"

"What worries me," her husband says, "is that Chávez is a populist of great ability. The masses love him, believe in him. But he's unprincipled and consumed by class resentment and hatred of the rich. Very dangerous guy."

Pedro, the butler, overhears this entire exchange, having already reentered the dining room holding a silver tray.

Observing the discussion, Carla asks, "Why don't you all listen to what Chávez has to say? Have any of you heard him speak or seen his campaign messages? Have you met him?"

She glances around the table. Martin stares at her with hostility, Olga and Doña Gabriela with disbelief. Her mother coughs and fidgets nervously in her chair.

"Carla, dear, can we talk about this some other time? says her husband. "Things might get out of hand here, you know?"

"No, Marcel. It's important we face reality. Three years ago, when I interviewed

Chávez in prison, he didn't impress me. I questioned his motives. Wasn't worth supporting, I thought—"

"And now you've changed your mind?" her sister interrupts. "Is that it? You must be joking!"

"I didn't realize he was a work in progress."

"And just how has he progressed, if I may ask?" says her brother-in-law, as he rolls his eyes.

"He's matured and surrounded himself with competent people, including some of our friends."

"Is that so?" Martin's sarcastic tone of voice conveys his doubts.

"Yes. But that's not the point. Chávez is genuinely concerned for the poor and is determined to fight corruption, the cancer eating away at this country."

Her husband sighs, shaking his head with a pained expression. "Carla, I don't think you'll get this crowd to support Chávez."

"But at least my family should know *I* do."

"Oh my God!" says Carla's sister.

"To be honest, I've been in regular contact with Chávez, helping with introductions and fundraising. Even convinced Marcel here," pointing to her husband, "to have his TV and radio stations endorse him."

"But he's communist!"

"You are mistaken, Olga. He is a socialist committed to ending inequality in our society, as we should all be. Our privileges have blinded us for too long."

She gets up and sings in the style of a Mozart aria. While singing, she walks around the table, stopping at each chair and putting her hand on the shoulder of the person there to make her message more personal.

37

Chávez Is Right

Why so much poverty,
In a land of wealth untold?
He asks the questions no one dares,
He speaks the truth. He cares.

Why so much injustice?
So much corruption?
So much suffering of our people?
Chávez is right.

He's fighting for those who have nothing
A cause worth fighting for.
Can he save this country?
I intend to find out.

When finished and seeing the shock on her mother's face, Carla goes over and nudges her to stand. "We should leave," she says.

"Marcel, could you please escort my mother out?"

"Of course," he replies, as he takes Doña Gabriela's arm.

The three take their leave. On the way, they intone a recitative-like dialogue, started by Doña Gabriela, with a single instrument accompaniment, such as a jazz tune played on a piano:

What Will My Friends at the Country Club Say?

Doña Gabriela: *¿Qué dirán mis amigas del Country Club?*
Carla: *Times are changing, mother.*
Marcel: *Chávez has much support at the Club.*
Doña Gabriela: *Imposible. No puede ser.*
Carla: *Times are changing.*
Doña Gabriela: *¿Qué dirán mis Amigas del Country Club?*

Now alone, Martin and Olga exchange glances. He scratches his head, and she shakes hers in disbelief, both struggling to make sense of the situation.

"How could this happen in our family?" she says. "My great-grandfather, General Julio Garrido, must be turning in his grave. My sister has no clue what she's getting into. The woman is crazy."

They sing to a Latin tune:

Carla Has Gone Crazy on Us

Olga: *¡Carla se nos volvió loca!*
What on earth happened to her?
She's lost her mind, it's clear as day
Does she believe what she just said?

Martin: *She's always the smart one,*
Now, thinks Chávez is the answer?
Has she forgotten who we are?
A traitor to her class, she is.

Olga and Martin: *Carla has gone crazy on us,*
What happened to her?
She's thrown away her senses,
She's driving us insane!

As they continue singing, they shift into dancing salsa in a subdued style, as becomes their social status.

Meanwhile, Pedro reenters the dining room, accompanied by the maids and cook, to clear the dishes off the table. Upon seeing the couple's graceful movements, the butler reaches out for Juana and mimics his employers behind their backs. Remberto does likewise with Salvadora. The four follow the rhythm with mock restraint and elegance, heads tilted up, eyes closed, and snobbish expressions on their faces.

Martin and Olga spot the dancers in the rear. Surprised, they, in turn, imitate the house servants—without restraint—knowing no one from their circle is watching.

Feeling liberated, they initiate a competition with the other couples to see which pair can perform the most outrageous and exaggerated steps.

The rivalry intensifies as the pace quickens, reaching a frantic level. Chaos erupts when the music grows more energetic, vulgar, and erotic. The choreography turns vigorous, hot, and acrobatic, with a rhythmic and seductive beat in the background, in the style of a lively piece by Billo's Caracas Boys. All are superb performers.

Martin leaps onto the dinner table, pulling Olga behind him, where the two gyrate body to body, turning tight and loose, in tune with the intoxicating Latin pulse. It's a wild, provocative show, with Olga's skimpy dress revealing her bare legs and red panties every time she spins. All traces of gentility vanish instantly.

Pedro and Juana soon replace them on the tabletop and continue to dance with even greater abandon and sensuality. But suddenly, they stop dancing, staying in place. First the butler and then the maid pump their clenched fists into the air while yelling with all their might: "Chávez, Chávez, Chávez, Chávez." Remberto and Salvadora are quick to join the unexpected outburst. Sharp staccato percussion and trumpet blasts punctuate the jagged arm movements and shouting.

In shock, Olga and Martin look up at the screaming house servants, their jaws dropping in astonishment.

FADE OUT

SCENE 7: ELECTION NIGHT TRIUMPH

OFFSTAGE NARRATOR: "Chávez wins his first presidential election after a hard-fought campaign, vowing to uplift the poor, eliminate rampant corruption, and bring prosperity and social justice to the country. He talks about a "Beautiful Revolution" to transform the nation. People believe him. Their day has arrived."

SETTING: Contemporary videos of this event flicker across the set's rear, showing hundreds of thousands of followers packed from wall to wall as far as the eye can see on the widest avenues of the city. They are waving flags, cheering, hugging each other, and jumping for joy. The size of the multitude is astonishing; the uproar of blaring horns, fireworks, shouting, and repeated singing of the National Anthem is overwhelming.

AT RISE: On a wide elevated platform spanning the entire stage, an excited group of VIP supporters, campaign officials, and other special guests await Chávez's victorious entrance. He will address the euphoric masses below (offstage), celebrating his landslide electoral victory. The attendees, dressed in red with tricolor caps (yellow, blue, and red), sit and stand on the structure as they wave to the crowds.

All sing a massive chorus, in the style of the "Triumphal March" from Verdi's *Aida*, about the immense hopes ordinary people have placed on this man, Chávez:

A New Dawn

A new dawn is upon us. Glory, glory!
The rebirth of our nation has arrived. Glory!
Chávez. Chávez. Chávez!
Our hero, strong and true!
Make Our Country Great Again.
Chávez. Chávez. Chávez.
The people rise with you!
Our day has arrived. Glory, glory!
A new dawn—Glory! Glory!

Carla and her husband, sitting at the front of the platform, are the only two not dressed in red. A spotlight shines on them.

"This is what you wanted, isn't it?" he says, raising his voice over the din. "We took a gamble, donated millions, and gave this guy unlimited favorable coverage on RVTV. We put him on the map. And here are the results: a resounding triumph."

"He will be a success. He has the best of intentions and a boundless capacity for work. The man is tireless. That I can attest to."

"Come on! The road to hell is paved with good intentions, don't you know that?"

"I am going to help him. He offered me a position in his cabinet. And I accepted."

"You **what**? You must be joking."

"No, you're looking at this country's next Minister of Communications."

He almost jumps out of his seat, pivoting to look at his wife. "Are you insane? One thing is to support this guy behind the scenes. It's another to serve in his administration."

"I have made many career choices long before I met you after graduating from Princeton. And the results have not been all that bad, don't you think?"

"I know. But there's a difference," he says, barely containing his annoyance. "I was just hedging my bets—trying to stay on the good side of whoever wins. That's it. But now you want to publicly tie yourself to this guy as a member of his cabinet? That's crazy. He could destroy all we stand for."

"But he's not going to. He wants a society where all share in the country's immense wealth. Not just a privileged few."

"You worry me, Carla. Those leftist ideas picked up in the Ivy League will turn you into a full-fledged socialist."

"Let's change the subject, OK? I intend to join the Chávez cabinet. Period."

After a long pause, she breaks the silence. "Did you spot Pedro and Jacinta? They're here as special guests, too."

"Of course I did. I remember he quit his job at your mother's house after an unpleasant incident. But I didn't know they worked for the campaign."

"Yep, believe it or not, they organized a very successful grassroots drive to mobilize the vote for Chávez in the barrios."

"Really?"

"Hundreds of thousands of poor people, who had never considered voting, went to the polls. It made a tremendous difference."

"So, do you think Chávez needed Pedro to win?"

"Quite possibly. I never suspected he had such organizing talents, and I am sure Chávez will reward him handsomely."

An immense roar from the vast multitude below drowns out their conversation. Chávez, followed by his stunning blonde, blue-eyed new wife, Maribel, climbs the steps to the platform with lightning speed. Guests swarm him, attempting to get as close as possible to touch and congratulate him.

Election Night, 1998

43

He extricates himself and faces the expectant public to start his speech, the first as president-elect, singing in a baritone in the defiant style of the "Toreador Song" from *Carmen*:

Before You a Humble Soldier

¡Mi pueblo! My people!
Before you, a humble soldier
Ready to serve until my final breath.
My destiny, if God so wills,
Is to fulfill your dreams,
The dream of Simón Bolívar,
A revolution of the people for the people.
A Bolívarian Revolution.
A Beautiful Revolution!

Celebrating with "mi pueblo."

Chávez continues in an exalted speaking voice.

"You, el pueblo, inspired by the spirit of Simón Bolívar, have given me a magnificent opportunity. And let me say loud and clear: I will not defraud you, I will not disappoint you, I will not abandon you. I will be here, my people, now and forever, at your side, a soldier of the revolution."

Massive eruption of cheers from below.

"I am but a straw in the wind. But together, we can be the storm that demolishes injustice and corruption in our society."

Carla and Marcel attempt to slip away as he says, "Jesus Christ! What bullshit. Let's go."

While trying to escape, they bump into Pedro and his wife Jacinta. A moment of awkwardness ensues, the former butler holding back in confusion. Hugging the daughter of his old employer, where he had been a house servant for over twenty years, embarrasses him.

Carla spontaneously embraces them while her husband looks on, frowning at the camaraderie with former servants.

"Great to see you both here on this special night!" she says.

"We heard you did important work for the campaign," Marcel says. "Congratulations."

"All we did was add our little grain of sand. That's all," Pedro says.

"More like truckloads of it. And the Comandante will be very grateful."

They struggle to have a conversation.

"Hard to talk here, with all these people, but let's keep in touch," Carla says.

"Of course, Señora Carla and Señor Marcel. And my regards to Doña Gabriela."

The crowd swarming about blocks the couple's exit. They have no choice but to listen to Chávez introducing his new wife to his jubilant supporters.

"Here with me is my beautiful Maribel. Aquí está." Chávez wraps his arm around her, both beaming.

45

"She, too, is part of this revolution. She is more than a First Lady. She's a combatant, the first combatant."

Cheers from below.

"Tonight, the two of us celebrate with el pueblo, with our brothers and sisters. But later, in private, I'm going to give her what's coming to her. I will give it to her!"

The cheers turn into wild shouting.

"And she loves it. Begs for it."

The throng erupts into a roar.

"I can't take this anymore," Marcel says as he pushes his way forward, pulling his wife past the people on the platform blocking the top of the stairs. They manage to climb down.

As they walk away, they make out the outline of a person, barely visible in the shadows, also exiting the celebration.

"Is that a guy up ahead, Carla? I hear his footsteps like he's pounding the pavement with unnatural force."

"And look at his outfit!" she says, "straight out of the 19th century, with his cloak, breaches, and riding boots. Is he going to a costume party?"

They quicken their pace to view the receding figure better as his strides become louder. Only a few yards behind the mysterious man, they witness a sight so startling that it brings them to a sudden halt.

He vanishes in total silence.

"Did you see that, Carla? Where is he? Incredible! Disappeared right before our own eyes. Or am I imagining things?"

"God knows! It's so dark. He might have made a sharp turn, and we didn't notice."

"No. We were too close for that. Would have seen it. And what happened to the loud footsteps? This is unbelievable."

"How did we wind up on this deserted street, anyway? Let's get out of here and find a busy intersection. This place gives me the creeps."

END OF ACT I

CURTAIN

ACT II

SCENE 8: CARLA RECEIVES A VIP

OFFSTAGE NARRATOR: "Carla has been Chávez's competent and hardworking Minister of Communications for the past three years. Her relationship with the president has been fraught with difficulties throughout her tenure."

SETTING: Carla is busy with paperwork at her desk in her well-appointed government office. Behind her, a formal portrait of President Chávez with the tricolor silk slash across his chest and the heavy solid gold links collar, symbols of his authority.

AT RISE: "The Minister of the Treasury is here, Señora Carla," announces her assistant over the intercom.

"Thank you. Let him in."

Pedro, the former house butler, enters the room, elegantly attired in an expensive gray suit with a striking red tie contrasting with his immaculate white shirt.

"Have a seat." She points to the modern black leather sofa while walking to the matching chair.

"Well, Pedro, and what brings you here today?"

"First, my sincere condolences for your mother's passing. I was very fond of Doña Gabriela, always kind and respectful to the help."

"Thank you. I appreciate you mentioning it."

"On a different matter, Señora Carla, I come to warn you that President Chávez is very upset with you. He is downright furious. To make things worse, many of his closest aides hate your guts, if you pardon my expression."

"I know. But I'm not signing those contracts. He can't seriously expect me to approve huge overprices, millions of dollars over the actual costs!"

"All I can tell you is that you run grave risks if you don't do his bidding. Being fired would be the least of it."

He moves closer to Carla's seat. "Chávez could shut down your husband's media empire. He is capable of ruining your entire family."

"Thanks for your concern. I promise I will think about it."

Her eyes meet his. "And what about you? How are things at the Treasury?"

"I am a simple, uneducated man. Didn't even finish high school. But running the Treasury is easy when money is plentiful, now that oil prices are going through the roof. We don't have any idea what to do with so much income."

"Same here. I understand what you mean."

"All day long, I sign checks as instructed by Chávez and his people. So many millions for Fidel in Cuba, so many millions for Bolivia, Argentina, and Nicaragua. You name it. Buying friends and allies is easy when you throw money at them."

She gazes at him without showing approval or disapproval.

"And, of course, I also transfer huge amounts to numbered Swiss accounts. None of my business where it goes. After all, they pay me handsomely for formalizing everything at the Treasury with my signature."

She shifts position in her seat, now uncomfortable with the turn in the conversation.

"Señora Carla, the rich in this country have been stealing public funds for generations. Time for the poor to do a little stealing as well, don't you think?"

"I suppose," she replies with a chilly tone, leaning back and distancing herself from the discussion.

"But one part of my job does keep me up at night. Worries me a lot!"

"Which part, Pedro?"

"All the money we send in cash, suitcases filled with it, to fake 'Human Rights Organizations,' fronts for terrorist groups. I can't understand it. Why would President Chávez support these criminals?"

"It's a complicated issue, which many of us who backed him in good faith are now learning. I do not have an answer, but there will be severe consequences for our country if we continue to aid terrorists."

They both get up.

"Once again, Pedro, thanks for your warnings. I'm going to take them seriously."

As he walks toward the exit, he turns around and says, "Señora Carla, do you have another minute? I would like to share one last memory from my time with the Garrido family."

"Of course, I would love to hear it."

They both remain standing.

"I was a new, young employee at your parent's house some thirty years ago when I witnessed an event that has stuck in my mind ever since."

"And what could that have been?"

"It was during your sister Olga's wedding celebration at the mansion. Your father, Dr. Garrido, was still alive. While I passed champagne to the guests, the orchestra struck up a beautiful waltz for the bride and father to dance before others joined them."

"Oh yes, I remember. It's the most sentimental part of the reception, where the father says farewell to his daughter, as he 'gives her away' to her new husband."

"Your sister looked splendid in her long white bridal dress, and Dr. Garrido so elegant in his formal wear. And then they danced."

Carla listens intently, as if transported to that day so many years ago.

"Imagine, Señora Carla, the impression it made on an ignorant young man from a dirt-poor family raised in a little village. The only dancing I had seen was joropo and merengues. For me, a waltz was something out of a fairy tale."

"A beautiful memory. Means a lot to me as well, because my father died soon after. I never got to dance with him on my wedding day."

"I have a confession to make," he says, looking embarrassed. "Now that I can afford it, I've been taking ballroom dancing lessons. I hope to be ready when the time comes to part with my only child, Josefa, when she marries."

He looks downward to hide his emotions. "I, too, want to waltz with the bride."

"Good for you, Pedro!"

She heads to the exit with him but stops. "I just got a terrific idea! How about if you dance a waltz right this instant with me, the daughter of Dr. Garrido, the bride's father who made such an impression on you."

"Oh, Señora Carla, I would never dream of such a thing!"

She goes to the credenza behind her desk, chooses a CD, and inserts it into the player, starting a beautiful rendition of "The Blue Danube," then walks over to Pedro.

"By now, you know a gentleman must ask the lady for the dance. I await your invitation, Don Pedro."

After a moment of hesitation, the former house servant moves closer and asks, "Will you do me the honor, Señora Carla?"

"I would be delighted."

The respectful, unassuming butler at the Garrido Bisset home takes Carla in his arms to dance "The Blue Danube," by Johann Strauss, skillfully, with surprising grace.

After the music stops, he says, "What a beautiful waltz, Carla!"

"There! You said it. Finally stopped calling me Señora Carla. Wasn't that difficult, was it?"

"I guess not. Not after that." He points to where they had just danced.

As he is preparing to leave, he says, "One last thing, which I meant to tell you. I was sorry to hear the family put up the Garrido mansion at the Country Club for sale after your mother's passing."

"Yes, we no longer had any use for it."

"Well, I bought it."

Taken aback, she quickly recovers. "Your turn to waltz, Pedro."

After he departs, she returns to her desk, head lowered as if burdened by her feelings. The anxious tone of her assistant on the intercom interrupts her thoughts. "It is President Chávez on the line, Señora Carla!"

She picks up the phone, and before she can greet the president, hears his unmistakable voice. "You are fired! Get the hell out of there right now!"

He hangs up.

FADE OUT

SCENE 9: SAMARA CONFRONTS CHÁVEZ AT THE PALACE

OVERHEAD SCREEN:
Presidential Office
January 2009

SETTING: Behind Chávez's large desk is a giant formal portrait of Simón Bolívar with colors so loud that it looks like the work of an auto paint shop. It is an overly decorated room with abundant patriotic symbols, flags, and long draped curtains cascading from the soaring ceilings. Overall decoration style: Grandiose Tastelessness.

To the side, toward the rear, is the familiar statue of Bolívar, which accompanies the Venezuelan president wherever he goes, including on his many trips abroad.

AT RISE: Chávez, wearing his customary red bulletproof shirt, is watching a large TV showing live coverage of the White House reception of Carla Garrido, by now the most prominent opposition leader, next to President George W. Bush and other distinguished guests at the Oval Office. Samara enters.

He angrily points to the screen and says, "Can you believe this shit?"

"Hugo, don't use obscenities in front of me! I won't tolerate it," addressing him like nobody else would dare.

"I know, I know, and I apologize. But it pisses me off—I mean, it annoys me—to see that woman, my former Minister of Communications, cozying up to that miserable drunkard, George Bush, and getting worldwide recognition."

He faces Samara. "No wonder that opposition group she heads has grown so much. The CIA finances it!"

"That's not the reason. People are tired of corruption, violence, human rights abuses, and fraudulent elections. You've become authoritarian, intoxicated with power."

55

Chávez ignores her, continues watching TV, still irritated, and says, "Carla has been a pain in the neck for the last few years as the most outspoken leader of everybody who hates me. Now that she has become an international celebrity, it will be harder to silence her."

"Why do that? Better to meet with her and her group and listen to what they have to say."

"What is this? You came here to tell me what to do like I am a schoolboy?"

"I care for you and the Beautiful Revolution. That's why I tell you the truth, something that nobody else around here bothers to do. They are all too busy filling their pockets."

He looks away from the screen, paying more attention.

"As to Carla … she worked for you faithfully, believed in your cause, and wanted to make your presidency a success. Until you fired her because she would not take part in your corrupt deals."

Their gazes meet.

"She is fiercely courageous, Hugo, the only person to dare confront you publicly. And on television! Remember that? When you were giving your annual speech to Congress?"

"I'd rather forget that little incident."

"It was amazing!" Samara says. "She rose from her seat to call out one of your many lies. Right there! In front of everyone and the cameras. Of course, what happened later was a disgrace. Some of your delegates assaulted her, and she was lucky to come out alive."

"Yeah, those idiots didn't finish the job. Got cold feet when they realized they were on a live broadcast."

"Hugo! It worries me when you say things like that. It has to stop." She leans over the table and places her hand on Chávez's forearm.

"Listen to me. I speak for the powers that rule our destinies. They will punish you

56

severely if you continue to betray your sacred commitment. Put an end to corruption. It's destroying your government. Do not lose your way, I warn you."

"Really?" Chávez says, his expression becoming quarrelsome. "Let me show you if I have lost my way! Let me show you what el pueblo, the real people—not oligarchs like Carla—think of me."

He leads Samara to the balcony of the presidential palace. Two guards open the doors, revealing the multitude below (offstage) awaiting the president in the early night hours. Powerful reflectors illuminate the scene. The crowd goes wild at seeing their hero, who vigorously waves his arms, allowing the cheers and shouts to subside before singing in the style of "Vivir Mi Vida."

Balcony of Miraflores

Take Me! Take Me! I Am Yours!

My people, my loves!
Mi Pueblo! Mis Amores!
I am yours now and forever!
Take me, take me!
I belong to you and only you.
I am your servant.
You command, and I obey.
When I stand here and feel
That immense love from you, my people,
I become like a mare awaiting the stallion!
Take me, take me! I am yours!

Samara shakes her head while leaving the balcony to await the end of the speech at an ornate chair by a faux Louis XV table.

When finished, Chávez, still exhilarated and full of adrenaline, sits down next to

57

her. "Did you see that? Did you see it?" he says. "You tell me now who's lost his way! El pueblo loves me. Can't get enough of me."

"Calm down, Hugo. Your underlings do not dare inform you that they pay people to attend your rallies, which nobody wants to go to these days. Who would want to listen to the same promises over and over again?"

"OK, something else must be bothering you, because it seems impossible to please you today. Why don't you read the cards to reveal what the Spirits have in store for me? They may be a little kinder than you."

"Yes, I will consult the Tarot. But before I do that, let me tell you what is on my mind. And it's very serious."

"Alright, what is it?"

"I heard you're planning to exhume the remains of Simón Bolívar, which ..."

Samara cannot continue, such is Chávez's reaction. He bolts from his seat, pushing away from the table with a loud scraping sound, as if he is about to flee, but stops to check the surroundings. After ensuring no one has eavesdropped on them, he sinks back into his chair.

"What's the matter, Hugo? Pull yourself together!"

Struggling to control his emotions, he says, "How on earth did you find out? Not a soul knows about it! Nobody. I haven't even told Fidel or any of my closest aides. It is my deepest secret. How did you find out? Tell me!"

She turns for an instant toward the Bolívar statue, a few yards away, which seems to tilt ever so slightly to face her. "Remember, my sources are not of this world! Olodumare, the Creator, sees all dimensions, past, present, and future. Hell and heaven. Good and bad."

She moves nearer, her eyes narrowed into an intense, aggressive expression. "Don't you dare touch the earthly remains of Simón Bolívar! Keep out! He will be ruthless with anybody who desecrates his bones."

Chávez watches her in silence, as if weighing her warning.

"I'm glad you understand the severity of this sacrilege," she says. "But let me also

58

caution you that if you persist in your corrupt ways and ignore the needs of our country, Bolívar is going to destroy you."

He stands, his movements becoming more self-assured as he defies her.

"For God's sake, Samara! Bolívar was buried almost 200 years ago. I am alive and kicking. What can he do to me? He is as dead as a doornail."

"Is he dead, Hugo?" She slams the table with her fist. "How could you, of all people, say that? Look me in the eye when you say it!"

She rises and moves toward him. Now side by side, she pours her indignation into a raw, angry song, such as: "Uprising."

Bolívar Lives!

Look into my eyes, Chávez!
How dare you deny his living spirit!
He raised you to the mountaintop,
Ungrateful man that you are!
Without Bolívar, you are nothing!
No, Bolívar is not dead—
Bolívar cannot die!

Chávez steps back, lowering and shaking his head, hands pressed over his ears to shut out her words.

Once finished singing, she closes in on him. "Tell me now! Is Bolívar dead?"

He does not reply.

Fuming with rage, Samara towers over him, then leans down, her face nearly touching his.

"I can't hear you! What is your answer?"

"Dead or alive, Samara, Bolívar won't stop me from reaching absolute power. I have to touch his bones to fulfill my destiny, and I will crush anyone or anything that dares oppose me. Even the Liberator."

FADE OUT

SCENE 10: EXHUMATION OF SIMÓN BOLÍVAR, OH HAPPY DAY!

OVERHEAD SCREEN:
Presidential Morgue
July 16, 2010

SETTING: Next to a long, stainless steel examination table is a pair of sturdy metal supports to place Simón Bolívar's heavy ceremonial coffin. Standing by are two forensic technicians in white coats and gloves in charge of the autopsy.

AT RISE: A welcoming committee of high-ranking officers and cabinet members, including Pedro and Gen. Velásquez, flanks President Chávez who says, "Let's sing together, everyone! Today, let's all be happy!"

All start singing the hymn "Oh Happy Day!" gospel choir style, clapping hands and rocking side to side, with the president as the lead singer. The arrangement of this religious song incorporates conga drums for a Latin touch. The link is for the original.

Oh, Happy Day!

Oh, happy day!
No sadness today!
Oh, happy day!
What joy!
Meeting Bolívar in person!
Two hundred years after his death!
Oh, happy day!

Chávez addresses the guests after the music stops. "This is not a disrespectful act! We are about to meet the great Simón Bolívar centuries after he died. Such an important event deserves a grand celebration!"

All nod in agreement as he says, "I have hired one of the most experienced musical groups in the world to escort our Liberator here. What a joyous occasion! Let the ceremony begin!" He snaps his finger at an aide.

Large double doors open at the back of the room to welcome a traditional New Orleans Jazz Funeral band in full swing, playing "When the Saints Go Marching In."

 The musicians roll their brass instruments and bass drum from side to side, in tune with the music. Behind them, pallbearers, dressed formally in top hats, carry Simón Bolívar's coffin, "dancing" it right and left and walking with the halting steps typical of these colorful processions.

New Orleans Jazz Funeral Band

After laying the casket on its supports, the bearers and ensemble exit to great applause and wild cheering from the guests. They all congratulate the president before quieting down to start the exhumation.

A solitary spotlight illuminates the coffin in the dimly lit room, creating strange and distorted shadows on the walls as the anxious bystanders move about.

The technicians get to work, struggling with the casket's 180-year-old lock. Just as they open it, a loud metallic crash startles them all.

Chávez and the rest run for the exit, but a guard—panting in fear—stops them. "Wait! Wait!" he says, trying to control his breathing. "It's just a heavy brass handle that fell to the floor. The wood is rotten."

Much relieved, the president recovers his composure and returns with the group to the side of the casket, where they await the painstaking removal of the layers of black silk fabric covering the cadaver. Long minutes pass before the workers unveil the content.

"There he is! In all his glory, the greatest man who ever lived," Chávez says, not in the least fazed by the sight of a bone-white, naked skeleton facing up with no remnants of flesh or clothes.

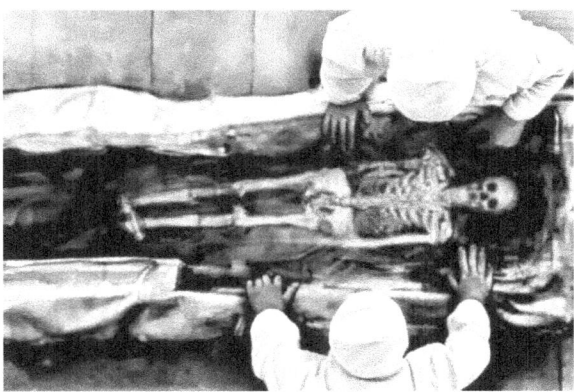

A "beautiful" skeleton

"Come closer, people. Isn't he beautiful? Look at him!"

The guests inch forward as if compelled to view a decaying carcass.

Pedro lingers longer than the rest and becomes agitated. "Comandante, did you see this? There is something by the side of Bolívar! What is that?"

Several in the group, including the president, go nearer.

An assistant points a flashlight at the item. "Seems to be a long feather quill pen," he says, "like they used in his lifetime. It's very well preserved, as if somebody had placed it there just days ago."

At first apprehensive, Chávez calms down as Pedro says, "Comandante, I don't think anybody would object if you keep it as a souvenir. You deserve it after all these wonderful arrangements."

The technician picks up the feather with a trembling hand, places it in a zip plastic bag, and offers it to the president, who hesitates to receive it.

"Presidente, accept it," says Pedro. "It belongs to you, a gift from Bolívar. It will make you happy for the rest of your life." Some attendees nod in agreement, while others exchange skeptical glances.

"Thanks. I appreciate the gesture, but now I would like to spend some time by myself with El Libertador. After waiting so many years for this moment, I want to share my thoughts with him in solitude."

The guests take the hint and file out.

At the door, Gen. Velásquez says to Pedro, his voice edged with anxiety, "This is wrong. It's against nature to disturb the dead. And it brings bad luck. I don't know why we are doing this." He exits with the rest as the room becomes gradually darker. <u>Ghostly music</u> drifts through the background.

Alone, Chávez approaches the casket, his steps resounding on the marble floor with a strange echo effect: *clack, clack*. He goes to the lower end, picks up a small bone from the foot of the skeleton, the big toe, and quickly tucks it away in his pocket.

Moving to the opposite side, *clack, clack* reverberations still following him, he stares at the bald skull.

With his left hand, he lifts it to eye level as if to have a personal conversation. In his deep baritone and with a somber intonation, he recites:

> *"To be, or not to be, Simón Bolívar.*
> *That is the question.*
> *Whether 'tis nobler to reincarnate Bolívar,*
> *Or suffer the slings and arrows of this life*
> *As a mere mortal.*

I hold your skull, Bolívar.
Dead you are. Oh, yes! Dead.
I live and breathe.
Glory, fame, and fortune await me.
Out of my way, Bolívar!
I am your replacement.
Nothing will stop my climb to power!
Not you, not God, not Satan."

He puts the cranium back in its place and pauses for a moment.

"What a farce," he says, his voice low. "I glorify Bolívar for the masses, but he means nothing to me. I'll soon shove him aside. He's my only rival for a place in history. And I will surpass him."

He heads toward the room's entrance, his steps echoing with the distinct *clack, clack, clack*. He stops when he hears muted whispers and creaking noises behind him.

"I don't know what that is, but I'm getting the hell out of here," he mumbles, his heart racing as he speeds up.

Suddenly, the heavy lid of the casket comes crashing down with a thunderous bang, dust bursting out of its sides. Startled, Chávez spins around. Utter shock overcomes him when he sees Simón Bolívar standing beside the coffin, his face showing intense anger with piercing eyes.

"How dare thou desecrate my remains, make a mockery of my very bones? And steal one for your sinister rituals!"

Bolívar gets closer.

"I ordered Samara to stop thee from committing this sacrilege and to end your corrupt ways. Yet thou ignored her. Now, thou shalt pay the consequences."

"And what are those?" he asks, his tone defiant and disrespectful. "What can you do? You're dead. You are in there!" pointing to the burial chest.

"I had thought better of thee, Chávez, than such dastardly treachery as this."

The Liberator grips the side of the coffin to contain his indignation.

"You are the past, Bolívar. I am the future! Your role on earth ended long ago. Mine is just beginning."

"Yes! And I had wished for thee to be my worthy successor. I attended your victory celebration and heard noble promises to the people. But now, thou hast become the most corrupt, incompetent, and arrogant leader I have encountered in over 200 years."

"I don't need your help. My powerful friends will make sure I succeed. And they are alive, not a shadowy, half-dead phantom, like you are."

Chávez strides forward, chest thrust out and shoulders squared. "Get out of the way, Bolívar! The world is my stage."

"I shall not step aside, thou imbecile! Thou dared break our sacred pact—to lead a beautiful revolution for the good of our people, to care for the poor, and to remain honest above all else."

"So what? Who gives a damn about your pact?"

"Arrogance is thy undoing. Soon, thou shalt face the penalty for thy deeds."

A spotlight narrows on the Liberator as he advances, raises his right arm with his palm facing Chávez, and proclaims:

"*I, Simón Bolívar, from the darkness of my resting place, cast upon thee a curse that shall bring forth your ruin. Cursed art thou, condemned to await execution at my command. Pain, suffering, and agony shall befall thee, as surely as night follows day.*"

The curse terrifies Chávez, a superstitious man. He trembles with fear, facing the formidable apparition, oblivious to the incessant knocking on the door.

Pedro opens it, peers in, and says nervously, "Presidente, we heard voices and were afraid an intruder had breached security. Are you alone, sir?"

Chávez goes toward the exit, hesitates, and glances back in search of Bolívar.

But nothing is there. Nada.

"Yes, yes, I am by myself," he replies almost inaudibly, still shaken.

"Sir?" Pedro asks, alarmed at not hearing anything. "What did you say?"

"I was reading verses from the Bible aloud," he says, trying to control himself while wiping cold sweat from his forehead. "Let us all leave so the pathologists can perform their autopsy."

He walks to join the others. The ghostly *clack, clack, clack* echo ebbs as he leaves the room.

FADE OUT

SCENE 11: TEARS IN MIRAFLORES

OVERHEAD SCREEN:
Presidential Office
October 4, 2012. Morning

SETTING: A distraught Chávez is at his desk, looking severely ill, as he wipes his feverish brow. He is bloated and bald from the effects of the crushing chemotherapy to treat the incurable cancer that devours his body.

AT RISE: Chávez asks his assistant over the intercom, "Did you call Maribel?"

"Yes, Señor Presidente. She should be here any moment now."

20 years after the coup d'état.

He attempts to read some documents but grows frustrated and flings them across the table with a gesture of impatience.

"¡Qué mierda!" he says aloud with anger in his voice. "I feel so miserable! My stomach is churning as if loaded with bricks, and I want to puke all the time."

He again reaches for the phone. "Where the hell is Maribel?"

"She's already here, Presidente. I will let her in right away."

The door swings open and his ex-wife strides in, attractive and slim at forty-eight, dressed in a navy-blue silk skirt suit, string of white pearls on her neck, and high heels. Friends had warned her about her former husband's shocking appearance, but she can barely contain her emotions seeing him so disfigured.

With considerable effort, Chávez stands up to greet her and sings in a subdued voice, joined by Maribel, in the style of the duet "The Prayer:"

I Don't Look So Good These Days.

Chávez: *I don't look so good these days.*
I see it in the mirror, feel it in my bones.
The shadows grow as hope fades away.

Maribel: *Hugo, you look fine.*
You're a strong man.
You've risen before,
And you can rise again.
You will beat this illness.

Chávez: *I'm not sure, Mari!*
I don't look so good these days.
Sometimes, I feel the end is near.
Closing in on me,
Silently, unstoppable
Like the sun sets before night.

Maribel: *The dawn always breaks,*
You will rise again,
No matter what it takes.

Chávez: *I don't look so good these days.*

Once finished, he walks with unsteady steps to a sofa and invites her to join him.

"I wanted so much to be with you," he says. "You are the only person I can confide in about my condition. You understand me, always have. I regret we divorced so many years ago."

Now on the verge of crying, he says, "I'm not going to make it this time. It's the end of the road for me." He sobs, leaning over to rest his head on her shoulder.

She cuddles him, as one might a grown child. Seeing this once arrogant, formidable man—often ruthless and evil—reduced to this pitiful and vulnerable state moves her. Tears well up in her eyes.

"You'll be just fine. I am sure of it!" she says, trying to sound convincing.

"You're lying, Mari. I am dying, and you know it. The best doctors in the world can't do a damned thing about it! My days are numbered."

"Have faith! Miracles happen all the time."

"Not when you are cursed like I am." He looks past her toward the Simón Bolívar statue in its customary place in the room. "An implacable, merciless curse. My death sentence. There is no escape!"

"Hugo, I don't share your beliefs in Santeria and your trust in Samara's prophecies. I am a Catholic and will pray for your recovery. You are going to live to see our daughter Rosines get married and have children."

"How is my little girl?" Chávez perks up, relieved to change the subject. "I love her so much! She is very special to me. I wish I could spend more time with her."

"She is doing well. A bright, cheerful teenager now. She's a good kid. Always talks about you, so proud of her dad."

"Remember why I insisted we name her 'Rosines'?"

"That was the name of your grandmother, no?"

"Yes." He squirms in his seat, his face flushed and sweaty as he recollects a painful memory.

"When I was a small boy, my mother was very strict with me, even cruel. She would scold me, chase me, and spank me hard with a belt. I was terrified!"

"Oh, it couldn't have been that bad."

"It was! I would run next door to my grandmother's house, crying for help. She would take me in her big arms and sometimes got hit herself while protecting me."

"You must be exaggerating. Mrs. Chávez is such a nice lady."

"Not to me, back then. The situation got so serious that I moved in with my grandma, and she raised me until I was a young man. The least I could do was to name our daughter after her."

"Why would your mother act that way? She so loves her other sons."

"I didn't understand it. Now, so many years later, I do."

"Maybe you were spoiled, a little brat."

"No, I wasn't. You see, my three brothers could pass for White. I am obviously mestizo. Bad hair, she would say, ashamed of me. Funny how she's grown to love me since I became president."

"Anyway, Mari, great to be with you. If I had to do it all over again, you would still be my wife."

"Hugo, we went through rough times. It was hard for me to deal with your infatuation with Fidel and your constant trips to Cuba."

Embarrassed and avoiding eye contact, he says, "That's all over now," and falls silent.

"Well, I see you're still wearing the Cuban Medal of Freedom he awarded you when you first met," she says to break the silence. "How is he, by the way?"

"One thing you can say about Fidel. He's realistic and down to earth. He'll take care of our country after …" At a loss for words, he says, "If something happens to me."

"Of that, I am sure," she says with heavy sarcasm.

"Yes, he has already designated Manduco as … my successor."

"Nicolás Manduco? Nicolás! The former bus driver? You must be joking!"

"No, I'm not. Manduco is the dumbest man alive, we all know. But he will do as Castro tells him. Fidel wanted a puppet, and he got it. A big one."

The intercom interrupts them. "Señor Presidente, your campaign staff is here waiting for you, and the motorcade is ready. What should I say?"

"That I am on my way."

Surprised, Maribel asks, "Where are you off to? You should get some rest."

"No, not now. Got to go to a huge rally this afternoon. A multitude will attend because it's the last event before the election. I can't let my people down. They are clamoring for me!"

"But it looks terrible outside, about to rain," she says, pointing to a window.

"You know what, Mari? Standing in front of an adoring crowd of hundreds of thousands shouting '¡Chávez! ¡Chávez! ¡Chávez! ¡El pueblo está contigo!' … that is the only medicine that works."

As if transformed into his old self, he becomes agitated and says, "It's like a surge of adrenaline, makes me believe I can conquer anything, that I will live forever!"

He embraces her. "Thanks for coming! It did me so much good. Let's get together again soon. And don't forget to give Rosines my love."

He strides away, leaving Maribel by the sofa, her head down, overcome with sadness.

FADE OUT

SCENE 12: LAST CAMPAIGN RALLY IN THE RAIN

OVERHEAD SCREEN:
Caracas City Center
October 4, 2012. Afternoon

OFFSTAGE NARRATOR: "On October 4, 2012, two decades after the unsuccessful coup d'état that brought him to fame, Chávez is holding the last rally of his fourth presidential campaign in the rain."

SETTING: The president addresses the ecstatic and rowdy masses below (out of sight). With his deep baritone, dramatic gestures, and even spontaneous dancing, he is an extraordinary performer who works up crowds like no other. Party and government officials stand behind him on the raised platform. Images of the contemporary event flash across the stage, showing it rained throughout the afternoon. Special effects simulate rainfall and occasional thunderclaps.

AT RISE: Chávez is swaying to the music blaring from the large outdoor speakers. When he starts his speech, he points to random people in the massive crowd—men, women, young and old—and exclaims that each of them is now Chávez. He infers he is going to die, but tells his followers never to give up the fight.

Last rally in the rain.

He breaks into a song in the style of "Make Them Hear You."
The large group of officials at the rear sing the chorus:

My Name Is Pueblo!

My name is Pueblo!
 I am no longer Chávez.
My name belongs to you,
To the voice of justice,
The cry for equality.
The struggle lives on!
It will never end,
  Will never die!
Chávez is Pueblo
Now and forever,
Eternal in your hearts!

A spotlight focuses on Samara and Pedro, standing next to each other on the raised stage. They talk as the music recedes.

"El Presidente looks energized today! Maybe he's not that sick, getting better," he says.

"Appearances are deceiving, Pedro. He is dying. This is his last public act. He won't be around for more than a couple of months."

Avenida Bolívar

"Yes, I know, but wish it wasn't true. It's so unfair. A man in his prime, who has so much to give the country and the world, struck down by that terrible disease."

"Most people see it that way. But that's not the reason. He brought it upon himself."

"What? The man has cancer, Samara. That could happen to anybody."

76

"He committed an unpardonable transgression. The Spirits warned him not to do it. But he defied them. Now he is paying the price."

"What are you talking about? What transgression?"

"Best not to get into details. Many others were involved."

Dread overcomes Pedro as he struggles to ask, "Is this about the exhumation of Simón Bolívar? Is that it?"

She attempts to leave without answering.

"Samara, explain what you mean!"

"What does that matter? It's all written in the stars. There is nothing you and I can do about it."

"About what? Tell me!"

Stepping away from Pedro, she once more tries to go.

He grabs her arm from behind, spins her around, and confronts her. "What do you know?"

She breaks free from his grip, but he blocks her path and shakes her arms in desperation, trembling with fear and disbelief. "What's the truth?" he pleads.

With a stern expression on her face, she fixes her eyes on him and says, "Everyone who witnessed the exhumation and desecration of Bolívar's bones will die within a year."

"But I was in the room…" he says in a voice barely audible, his mind struggling to comprehend what he has just heard.

"Yes, and there is nothing I can do."

She walks away, leaving Pedro gasping for air, stumbling with his arm outstretched, looking for something to lean on.

FADE OUT

SCENE 13: CNN'S HENDERSON SCOOPER INTERVIEWS CARLA

OVERHEAD SCREEN:
Carla Garrido's Residence
October 5, 2012

OFF STAGE NARRATOR: "Carla is under house arrest at her apartment in one of the more affluent neighborhoods of Caracas. Security is lax, which allows her to receive visitors often, including journalists like Henderson Scooper of CNN."

SETTING: Carla's living room reflects her sophisticated modern taste, with understated yet valuable furnishings and décor. The space is airy and filled with light.

AT RISE: Carla welcomes Scooper as he enters her living room. She shakes his hand and asks him to sit.

"Good to see you again, Henderson!"

"Same here. Can you believe it? It's been over seven years since I interviewed you in Washington after you met with President Bush. I remember your husband was also there. We had a great conversation. He's a very bright guy. How is he, by the way?"

"Marcel and I separated two years ago, and he now lives in the US. He had a rough time when Chávez shut down his TV stations and newspapers. And I am partially to blame."

"Sorry, didn't know anything. Public life does take a toll on marriages and families."

"Anyway," she says after an awkward pause, "what did you think of the campaign rally yesterday? I know CNN came here to cover it."

"The outpouring of support for Chávez was overwhelming. He will be reelected and, frankly, that's the best outcome. He's done a lot for this country."

"Like what, Henderson? Haven't you heard of the scandalous corruption in his administration? The billions stolen? Money that should go to help the poor, not to

79

mention the atrocities and violations of human rights."

"Carla, whenever a popular leader uproots the ruling elites, often corrupt themselves, there is fierce pushback from those shoved aside."

"Might seem that way to you from afar. But here on the ground, it's a different story. Once the richest nation in Latin America, we are on the verge of collapse, while Chávez bankrolls a worldwide network of corrupt, anti-democratic regimes and terrorists."

"Do you have proof of that?"

"Of course I do! I will gladly send you some incriminating intelligence reports, some from your own services."

"Please do, because I am not convinced."

The accompanying camera crew finishes setting up the lighting panels for the recording.

"You're due at the airport soon to fly back to New York. So let's start the interview, shall we?"

Henderson begins. "You once supported President Chávez and were a key cabinet member. Now, you are his fiercest, most outspoken critic and lead an influential group working to oust him from office. What happened?"

"Many, like me, backed him in good faith. But as he accumulated absolute power, he became corrupt, authoritarian, and dangerous."

20 years after the coup d'état.

"How so?"

"Chávez was obsessed with becoming the leader of all the radical, anti-American, and autocratic countries in the world. He provides weapons and millions to terrorists in every continent. All of this stems from his intimate—and I mean really intimate—relationship with Castro, a declared enemy of the US."

"So why is he revered by the less fortunate in this country, the common people? The working class adores him."

"That's typical of all populist despots in Latin America. While funding is available, you throw it at the poor with subsidies, handouts, and public programs, all plagued with graft and corruption."

She pauses to look him in the face. "But some money trickles down to the impoverished, who think it will last forever."

"And it doesn't, of course," he says.

"No, and we're headed toward complete chaos once resources dry up. It's catastrophic."

"If that is your opinion, how do you see the future of this country?"

"Complicated. Chávez is terminally ill and will not survive more than a few months. But his movement won't die with him. And it's going to get much worse for our people."

"Sounds like you are pessimistic."

"No, I'm realistic—it's a long road ahead. I understand the challenges. Success isn't guaranteed, but we have to try."

"Are you talking about years or decades? Do you plan to seek the presidency someday?"

Carla gets up, resting her hand on the back of her chair, and while the reporter looks on, sings in the style of <u>Ombra mai fu</u> by George Frideric Handel:

**Democracy Is a Journey,
Not a Destination.**

Democracy is a journey,
Not a destination.
We've only just begun,
Each step is slow and steep,
Failures blocking our path,
Successes inspiring us.
No matter how long or far this road extends,
Our journey toward democracy never ends.

When she finishes singing, Scooper and his crew get ready to leave.

He stands. "You are very dedicated and determined, but you face a tough task—some would say impossible."

With an unwavering gaze, Carla replies, "My only goal is to restore freedom, regardless of the sacrifice. If I succeed, millions stand to benefit. If I fail, I'll take pride in risking everything for it. That's my reward."

"Carla, you have a will of steel. No wonder they call you the 'Iron Lady' around here. I deeply respect you, even if we don't see eye to eye on Chávez."

"Yes, many in Europe and the US, like you, view him favorably. Time is going to prove all of you wrong.

"Well, I'm not so sure about that. Troubled Latin American countries need a 21st-century version of socialism to achieve an equitable society. President Chávez had it right, but his illness cut him short."

He and his crew move toward the exit.

"I still wish you luck with your plans, and I mean it," he says as he shakes her hand. "I know many want a peaceful transition. Unfortunately, in this country that doesn't work. Goodbye, Carla."

FADE OUT

SCENE 14: DEATH IN LA HABANA

OFFSTAGE NARRATOR: "Hugo Chávez is terminally ill at the elite hospital reserved for the Castro family and high-ranking government officials."

SETTING: The patient occupies a suite with a spacious bedroom and an adjoining visitors' area separated by a doorway. Both spaces are visible to the audience.

AT RISE: Fidel Castro enters the room, dressed in fatigues and looking aged. A physician in a white coat, stethoscope around his neck, confers at a table with a tall, black-haired, mustachioed man, Nicolás Manduco, vice president of Venezuela. The two rise to their feet.

"How is the jerk next door?" Castro asks.

"President Chávez is resting just now," says the doctor. "He's been more animated and alert. His two older daughters visited him yesterday."

"Is that so? Is he getting better?"

"Oh no, Comandante. Since there is nothing we can do for him anymore, we administered powerful painkillers and stimulants to make his remaining days more tolerable."

"I see," he says with total indifference, his mouth opening wide to unleash a massive and prolonged yawn.

"We also wanted him to say goodbye to his loved ones. He keeps asking about you, wants you to come and visit."

"I don't have time to waste on a man on death row. Tell him I am traveling and due back soon, or whatever you want. I'm sick and tired of Chávez."

Castro orders the doctor to leave. "I need to talk to Manduco in private."

In the adjacent bedroom, a medical technician, clipboard in hand, monitors the equipment tracking Chávez's vital signs. He checks that the patient is sleeping and that they are alone. Then, he adjusts a knob on a large screen displaying a heart rate graph, changing it to a live broadcast of a baseball game. Without making a sound, he stays rooted to the spot, cheering with an upraised arm and a clenched fist.

In the visitor's room, Castro looks at Manduco. "Chávez is about to kick the bucket, damn it!" He strikes the table with his palm. "And we have so much unfinished work to do! Drug shipments, money transfers, documents to falsify, people to imprison. Couldn't that idiot just hold on for a few more months?"

"Don't worry, Comandante. I have a plan."

"You better, if you know what's good for you. I'll keep you in power as long as you do as I say and pay up every month."

"Yes, yes. I would not survive for a day without the help of your intelligence services. I guarantee you millions in free oil. Count on it."

"OK. So, what is your plan?"

"Doctors expect Chávez to die before the end of this December. We need him around until at least March of next year to get his signature, if you know what I mean."

"So?"

"After he dies, we freeze-dry him and send him back to Caracas. But we claim he is alive and receiving treatment there."

Castro leans forward, showing greater interest. "Then what?"

"We conceal his death completely until we are ready to announce it. What do you think?"

"Well done, Manduco! You are not as dumb as you look. I am going to have hospital staff summarily shot if they leak the truth. You had better do the same with your people."

"Comandante, I am not at liberty to shoot whoever I want like you. I wish I could. I have to bribe them to keep silent. But that works too."

"Maybe so, but it's a lot cheaper my way."

The dictator rises and opens the door to check on Chávez, who lies on his side, a frail hand shielding his shockingly aged face and bald head.

Spotting the technician absorbed in the baseball game, he summons two bodyguards. They approach the lab worker from behind, grab him under the shoulders and hurl him facedown onto the floor. A guard places his boot on his neck. The other leans down and warns the captive in a furious, loud whisper,

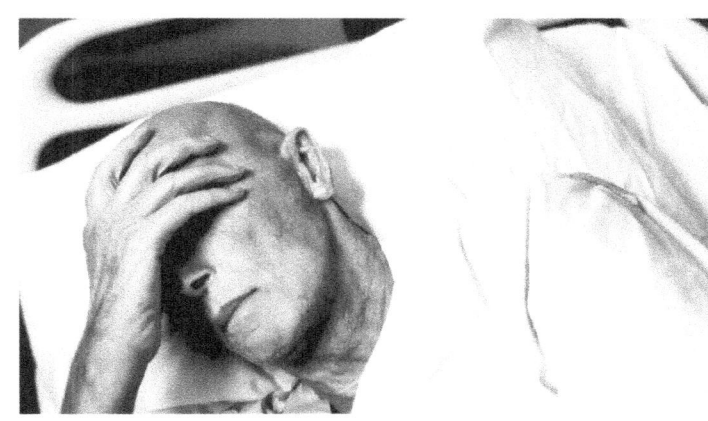

Near Death

"Stay silent, or you're dead." They drag him away,

Castro returns to the table as if nothing had happened and says, "I saw a sculpture of Simón Bolívar in a corner. What's that doing here, Manduco? This is not a goddamned museum. This is a respectable hospital."

"Sorry, Comandante. We had to indulge the president. Bolívar travels wherever he goes. I suppose we'll bury it with him."

"I don't give a shit what you do with that statue or Chávez after we vacuum-freeze him. But never let me catch sight of Bolívar again. This is Cuba, ¡coño! We don't need liberators here. Is that clear?"

"Yes, sir!"

Once the two men leave, the Bolívar figure comes to life and walks toward the bed where the patient sleeps, his hand covering his face. Bolívar unceremoniously shakes him awake.

"Did you think I would forget thee, Chávez?"

85

"Oh my God, Generalissimo! My prayers answered. I so much wanted to see you, to talk to you, to come to an understanding. Only you can save me now."

"When last we met, you dared defy me, no? Desecrated my remains, mocked our sacred pact. Believed thyself invincible. Behold thee today, wretched man."

"Sir, I was drunk with power. It went to my head. But I have learned from my mistakes and am ready to start over again."

"Fool! Thou knew the punishment for breaking the solemn treaty we forged, and cast aside the honor to be my worthy successor."

Bolívar moves to the foot of the hospital bed, grips the guardrail, and leans forward toward the terrified Chávez.

"I accuse thee of treason—of betraying our Beautiful Revolution, our people, our children, our poor, our future. And for what? False glory and fleeting riches? What difference shall that make when thou soon liest rotting in thy grave?"

"Sir! Sir! Give me a second chance, for the love of God. Lift your curse, I beg you."

"I come not to pardon, but to hear the last words of a condemned man."

Chávez cowers, pushing back against the pillow while pulling the sheet closer to his face as if to hide from Bolívar's wrath.

"Thou wert the chosen one to lead my people out of the wilderness of poverty — yet thou hast led them down a path of ruin."

"Generalissimo, have mercy on me!"

When Chávez sings, and Bolívar joins him, a duet ensues in the style of "Au Fond du Temple Saint" from a Georges Bizet opera.

Give Me a Second Chance

Chávez: *Give me a second chance, Bolívar!*

Bolívar: *Second chances are not for those who betray. You abandoned your people.*

There's a price you must pay.

Chávez: *I'll redeem myself, rebuild what I tore,*
And lead us to glory as never before!

Bolívar: *I gave you a noble path to tread,*
No more chances once that path is dead.

Chávez: *Bolívar! Spare me this fate!*
A second chance is not too late!

Bolívar & Chávez: *We cannot escape our fate.*
Bolívar! Bolívar!
All is written in the stars!
Bolívar! Bolívar!
There is no release from the past.
Your destiny is cast.

Chávez collapses onto the bed, his face contorted with pain, exhausted and struggling to breathe.

Bolívar moves closer. "Time to extract my punishment," he says.

Sobbing, Chávez seeks a sign of compassion, reaching out to touch Bolívar with a trembling, emaciated arm. "Bolívar, Bolívar, have mercy!"

"No! I am going to prolong thy suffering for weeks until you beg me to end thy misery. But I shall not."

"Thou shall die in agony, Chávez!"

Bolívar lingers at the bedside and hears Chávez, his face buried in his pillow, cry and plead, "Mama, mama, please don't hurt me. No me pegues, mami."

Contemptuous of this display of weakness, the Liberator turns and departs with his back to the audience. A solitary light pierces the darkened stage, tracing his steps as he fades into the distant shadows of his past.

OFFSTAGE NARRATOR: "Hugo Chávez died in La Habana on December 28, 2012. Castro ordered his body flown to Caracas, ostensibly to continue treatment. The vice president of Venezuela proclaimed his death over two months later, on March 5, 2013."

THE END

AFTERWORD

THE NIGHT I HAD A DRINK WITH HUGO CHÁVEZ
Where It All Began

SIMÓN BOLÍVAR & CHÁVEZ
An Obsession and the Myth of Faust

HUGO CHÁVEZ
Millions Adored Him, Millions Wished Him Dead

WHY A MUSICAL?
Another Country, Another Life, Same Story

A HYBRID FORMAT
Short Novel and Stage Play Combined

ACKNOWLEDGMENTS
My Appreciation to Friends & Family

THE NIGHT I HAD A DRINK WITH HUGO CHÁVEZ

Where It All Began

I first met Chávez in early 1998 at the apartment of Luis Miquilena, an experienced political operator who became his mentor. He convinced the former insurrectionist Lieutenant Colonel to run for office rather than seek power by military means. More than any other man in the country, Miquilena helped Chávez win the presidency of Venezuela in December of that year.

It was a curious and revealing meeting, the seed for this musical written decades later.

Chávez's campaign was gaining traction as he ardently criticized the democratically elected administrations preceding him. He did not spare the sitting president, Rafael Caldera, who had pardoned him and commuted his prison sentence. Miquilena, a veteran of many political movements, including the Communist Party in his youth, guided and restrained his strong-willed disciple.

"Avoid being too formal with Hugo. He prefers to be called by his first name."

When I contacted Miquilena through a mutual friend, he asked me to be at the entrance of his building, in a well-to-do residential sector of Caracas, at 9:00 p.m. on the appointed date. He and the candidate would arrive a bit later. Avoid being too formal with "Hugo," he advised me. "Don't get too elegant on him. He prefers to be called by his first name."

I waited in silence in a small living room as Mrs. Miquilena promptly returned to watching her telenovela nearby after letting me in. So scarce were funds at that stage of the campaign that the future president had to share Miquilena's cramped apartment, which doubled as their command post.

Shortly after 10 p.m., I heard voices outside the doorway. Miquilena and the candidate walked in with a single bodyguard, later known for his expensive designer clothes while preaching socialism as a legislator. His yellowish eyes, set in a face scarred by long-gone acne, left a lasting impression on me. *Central casting for the bad guy,* I thought.

Miquilena made the introductions while serving drinks, Chávez barely touching his after raising his glass to his lips for a courtesy toast. Drained from an exhausting day of campaigning, he stretched backward on the sofa, with his arms crossed above his head, struggling to suppress a yawn.

The host explained I was president of a nonprofit association for the defense of free enterprise in Venezuela, with over 1,000 corporate and individual members, including many prominent businessmen. Like other industry groups, we were concerned about the lack of clarity in Chávez's economic policies, suspecting him of being a socialist. In short, the candidate needed to meet with influential business and professional sectors to broaden his base of support.

Chávez did not seem very interested when Miquilena asked me to describe to "Hugo" what I had in mind. My proposal was a tried and tested formula for aspiring candidates: a schedule of working breakfasts with only thirty or forty people in attendance, followed by a "Q&A" period to allow the guest speaker to explain his position in greater detail.

Miquilena immediately approved the idea, seeing it as a potential source of campaign donations. The Lt. Col. flatly rejected it, saying he had no time to meet with Alvaro's "friends." He then quoted a biblical passage, which he later made famous: "Those with eyes shall see. Those with ears shall hear." His straightforward and tactless reaction surprised me, but I realized he was being honest. Hypocrisy, I concluded, is an acquired taste of more experienced politicians.

In contrast, Miquilena apologized during our shared elevator ride to the ground floor. He explained Hugo was tired and in a bad mood after a long day, but would soon understand the benefits of approaching the private sector. As we parted on the sidewalk outside his building, he told me they would follow up on my proposal.

And that they did. I received a call shortly afterward from General Alberto Müller Rojas, the newly designated manager of the campaign. He wanted to know when we could schedule the first breakfast. I made up an excuse and informed the disappointed general that the breakfasts would no longer be possible. There was, of course, a reason for aborting the plan—a powerful one.

Just a couple of days after my meeting at Miquilena's, I attended a party at a friend's house who, much later, would join the opposition to the Chávez government. Admiral Radamés Muñoz León, a tall, imposing former defense minister with an air of authority, was there. He knew of my overtures to the leftist candidate and asked if I had listened to his intervention at La Universidad de la Habana four years earlier. It was Chávez's first appearance abroad after getting out of prison, and Fidel Castro, his host, was there, paying close attention to his new protégé. I confessed I was unaware of it. The Admiral said he would have a copy of the recording delivered to me the next day (this was before forwarding videos).

The speech was a deal-breaker.

It's available on YouTube, so I will not elaborate here. Most alarming was the adulation of Fidel and his regime, the ruin of generations of Cubans. The recently freed insurrectionist rehashed the stale accusations of the ruthless exploitation of Latin America at the hands of industrialized countries, especially the behemoth up North. Later, Chávez often used these grievances, a cornerstone of his political ideology, to rally support and justify his socialist policies.

The video stunned me, for I despised Fidel Castro and everything he represented: the oppression of his people; imprisonment, torture, and execution of adversaries; the devastation of the Cuban economy; massive theft of public funds; and the millions of exiles. All caused by his record-breaking years as an absolute, unelected tyrant, followed now by his brother Raul, still holding onto power behind the scenes. And a younger generation of the family awaits in the wings. Cuba today is a bankrupt, tropical communist monarchy.

Which brings me to a pressing question: Why do so many celebrities, intellectuals, filmmakers, and world leaders idolize this murderous tyrant and his oppressive

> *"Why do so many celebrities, intellectuals, filmmakers, and world leaders idolize Castro, a murderous tyrant?"*

regime? This fascination with Fidel Castro strikes me as a disturbing pathology rooted in hysterical anti-Americanism and, more significantly, a romanticized worship of the ultimate antihero. To these VIP admirers of Castro, it seems "cool" and daring to turn against the very democratic values that enable their freedoms, fame, and wealth. Ironically, not one of these foreigners would last a moment under the brutal realities of a Cuban-style dictatorship.

Consider this: The recognition bestowed on a person who has the world's most famous religious figure knocking at his door and, upon entering, going to the living room, where the illustrious visitor sits, holds hands, and exchanges gifts with the elderly host. Family and grandchildren everywhere, of course. A cozy reunion, no less, missing only the hotdogs, hamburgers, and french fries.

I refer to the late Pope Francis's visit to the home of Fidel Castro in September 2015. Whoever receives such an immense honor from God's "representative" on earth has every right to feel accepted, legitimized, and vindicated in front of the entire world. All is forgiven. Or perhaps the distinguished guest thought there was no need to forgive his host's long, bloody career.

> *"The Pope's visit to Castro felt like divine absolution. If the Pontiff was truly that compassionate, he could have laid a wreath on Pinochet's tomb, to even things out."*

If the Pontiff was truly that compassionate, I would have respectfully suggested he lay a wreath on Augusto Pinochet's tomb to even things out a bit.

SIMÓN BOLÍVAR & CHÁVEZ
An Obsession and the Myth of Faust

A highly popular US president, and passionate admirer of George Washington, successfully promotes a constitutional amendment to change the country's name from the current United States of America to "The Washingtonian Republic."

Absurd?

That is precisely what the late President Chávez did in Venezuela in 1999. He added the surname of the independence hero and founding father of the country, Bolívar, to the official designation of the nation. This alone reflects the depth of an obsession that would lead to the televised exhumation of the remains of

> *"Chávez, many said, wanted to view and touch Bolívar's bones following his beliefs in Santeria, the Afro-Cuban religion."*

the South American liberator to investigate if local "oligarchs" had poisoned him almost two hundred years prior. Such was the public explanation. Others think differently. Chávez, many said, wanted to view and touch the bones following his beliefs in Santeria, the Afro-Cuban religion. This bizarre yet real-life incident gave rise to the "Curse of Simón Bolívar"—the superstition that anyone who disturbs Bolívar's corpse will suffer grave misfortune. It is at the heart of this story.

In this musical, I have reimagined Chávez's complex emotional and ideological bond to the nation's founder as a Faustian pact. Over the centuries, there have been many versions of this tale, but at its core is the legend of a man who sells his soul to the devil for knowledge and power. The primary themes focus on ambition, temptation, and damnation.

Here, Chávez and Bolívar are the protagonists of the ancient German myth, which I flipped on its head. The all-powerful representative of the devil, Mephistopheles, becomes a God-like Bolívar, a force for justice and retribution reminiscent of Jehovah in the Old Testament. He commands Chávez, in the role of Faustus, to honor his oath to serve his people faithfully and resist corruption in exchange for the presidency.

> *An angry Bolívar to Chávez: "Thou wert the chosen one to lead my people out of the wilderness of poverty — yet thou hast led them down a path of ruin."*

The penalty for breaching this pledge is an excruciatingly painful death, meted out by a wrathful Bolívar. As the final judgment looms, Bolívar accuses a desperate Chávez: "Thou wert the chosen one to lead my people out of the wilderness of poverty — yet thou hast led them down a path of ruin."

While this work presents a fictionalized Bolívar, historians consider the real man one of Latin America's greatest minds. In his day, he was internationally renowned, and his stature continues to grow. He personified a rare combination of military prowess, prophetic vision, and intellectual heft. As a result, his life and work have reached mythical proportions among the people of his continent.

A romanticized and sanitized portrayal of Bolívar's revolutionary career shaped Chávez's movement and thinking as early as his days as a cadet. Later, as president, Chávez elevated the independence hero to a sacred status for political gain. Exalted nationalism was a key element in Chávez's speeches about eradicating the existing world order to create an equitable society. He used a prestigious "brand," Bolívar, to market the same shopworn, populist jargon of all leftist Latin American politicians.

HUGO CHÁVEZ

Millions Adored Him, Millions Wished Him Dead

Few recent political figures have stirred so much worldwide controversy. From humble beginnings, Hugo Chávez became the virtual dictator of Venezuela, controlling all the major institutions: from the military to the legislature, from the press to the

> *"Consumed by his addiction to power, everything he did was to satisfy his hunger for control."*

Supreme Court. Consumed by his addiction to power, everything he did was to satisfy his hunger for control.

It all began with the failed coup d'état of 1992. Inexplicably, his captors allowed Chávez, the leader of the insurrection, to address the nation after they apprehended him. Troops loyal to the government had defeated the insurgents, but sporadic combat remained. The officers who detained the Lt. Col. instructed him to order any rebels continuing to fight to lay down their arms to avoid further bloodshed— and on live TV! They granted him the opportunity of a lifetime, which he skillfully exploited with an unsuspected talent for improvisation under pressure. And what a performance it was.

Staring fearlessly at the cameras, surrounded by throngs of journalists, Chávez gave his famous "Por Ahora" (for the time being) one-minute speech, remarkable for its boldness and bluntness. Delivered under the most stressful conditions, that sudden broadcast propelled the unknown officer to national fame. It was a turning point in Chávez's meteoric political career, culminating in four presidential elections, all but the first denounced as fraudulent by impartial, outside observers.

Some of his comrades later accused Chávez of cowardice for hiding in a military museum while his men were still fighting. But his brief public appearance that night gave the opposite impression. It showed a man in complete control of his emotions, taking responsibility for the rebellion and proclaiming that the insurgents had not met their objectives "for now."

In his initial campaign of 1998, he received support from the middle and upper classes—prominent businessmen, politicians, and media moguls. Most importantly, he had the resounding backing of the impoverished and marginalized in a country where authorities describe this segment, the vast majority, as "las clases populares."

The future president expressed outrage about corruption in the previous administrations. He condemned mismanagement of the immense oil resources of Venezuela, the most prosperous Latin American nation of that era.

His message? Inexcusable misery in an ocean of wealth—a powerful narrative that resonated with many people in all sectors, including me. The skyrocketing crime rate and deteriorating living conditions plaguing large portions of society were alarming. But the wealthier classes, which led comparatively privileged lives, were clueless, sitting on a ticking time bomb without the faintest idea of what was happening underneath them.

Chávez, a charismatic populist of exceptional ability, had a remarkable emotional connection with the masses. His speeches, interviews, radio and TV programs, and off-the-cuff remarks were down-to-earth, natural, spontaneous, laced with profanities and, above all, in the manner of ordinary people. His deep baritone conveyed conviction and authority. Yet, behind the charm and warmth, he was an unprincipled, ruthless, and diabolical man capable of systematic deceit. Class resentment and hatred toward the White elites, the "oligarchs," consumed him because of his low social standing and mixed-race background.

Was the controversial president a "closeted" gay man, as some have insinuated?

> *"Was the controversial president a 'closeted' gay man, as some have insinuated?"*

Individuals around him were, but there is no proof that Chávez himself was gay. This work, however, takes ample artistic liberties in this regard, as it does with Fidel Castro, accused of many things but not, to my knowledge, of homosexuality. The explicit intimacy between the two men dramatizes a relationship that became parasitic, with the Cuban autocrat exerting total dominance over a subordinate head of state. And all to the benefit of Cuba's decadent regime, saved from economic collapse by multimillion-dollar subsidies from Venezuela while its own people went hungry. The Cuban tyrant never stopped receiving his millions, even as homeless kids ate from piles of garbage on the streets of Caracas.

Once in office, Chávez's extreme socialist agenda, under the guise of a "Bolivarian" movement, or a "beautiful revolution," as he would often say, destroyed the economy. The arbitrary expropriations of businesses and private property alienated the professional and business community, which viewed the government as communist. Corruption reached unprecedented levels, making the scandalous theft of public funds that preceded it look like shoplifting by comparison.

As he consolidated his grip on power, the populist leader exploited the pent-up frustration among the poor with the pervasive social and economic inequality. Class conflict and rabid anti-Americanism fueled his "Socialism for the 21st Century," a source of inspiration for many other countries.

On the international scene, the polarizing president of Venezuela squandered the country's vast oil wealth to bolster the economies of corrupt governments in Latin America and to subsidize terrorist groups around the globe. He formed close alliances with notorious authoritarian regimes, most notably Castro's Cuba and the Islamic Republic of Iran. "Tell me who your friends are, and I will tell you who you are" is a tailor-made proverb for this man.

At the height of his power, Chávez believed he was invincible and ignored his cancer and the warning signs of the mounting problems facing his government. When the incurable disease killed him in La Habana in 2012, the widespread corruption and systematic destruction of the private sector had driven this once prosperous nation over the edge and into utter ruin. Almost single-handedly, he transformed inner cities into scary, apocalyptic, no-man's-lands with electrical blackouts, kids starving in the streets, and the sick dying in hospitals for lack of medicines. Worse yet, under Nicolás Maduro, the current, entrenched autocrat handpicked by Fidel Castro, this strategically important country became a rogue state and international safe harbor for terrorists, guerrillas, and narco-generals.

The result was an exodus on a scale never seen before in South America or anywhere else in the world during peacetime. Over 25 percent of the population, starting with the well-to-do and later encompassing all strata of society, has fled, desperate to seek a better life elsewhere. Today, millions of stigmatized and unwelcome immigrants struggle outside their homeland, a tragic consequence of Chávez's rule.

The damage is irreversible. Most trained professionals left and continue to leave Venezuela, never to return after more than a quarter of a century of "chavismo." Young people with promising careers ahead of them and much to contribute to their own country are now middle-aged, dispersed all over the world, where some have become valuable members of their adopted communities. Their children and grandchildren barely speak Spanish.

> *"We look back with nostalgia to the democratically elected governments that preceded Chávez as if they were a forty-year success story. They were not."*

Venezuelans have a well-earned reputation for short memories. Borderline amnesia, I would say, as a native of Caracas, the capital. So catastrophic was the Chávez era and its current sequel that we look back with nostalgia to the democratically elected governments that preceded it as if they were a forty-year success story trampled by the insurrectionist Lt. Col. They were not.

What came before Chávez was a self-perpetuating, deeply flawed, corrupt system controlled by two parties that alternated sharing the loot and power. Yes, they held elections, but each successive government was worse than the one before it. Only the economic, political, military, and social elites benefited. In contrast, the overwhelming majority of the population lived in impoverished rural areas or overcrowded, unsanitary, crime-infested slums with minimal or no public services.

There would have been no Hugo Chávez had previous administrations been reasonably competent and honest. Far from it. The often-cited forty years of democracy, celebrated as the country's golden era, were the fertile breeding ground for the Lt. Col. and his cohorts. And Venezuela and its people are still suffering the tragic consequences.

WHY A MUSICAL?
Another Country, Another Life, Same Story

The former Venezuelan president's disastrous impact on his country plunged millions into something akin to the aftermath of civil war. And yet, after his death at fifty-eight from a voracious strain of cancer, he remains popular—indeed, venerated—in much of Latin America and beyond.

The cult of Chávez in the poor and marginalized masses mirrors that of another populist, Evita Perón, who died at thirty-three, also of cancer, three-quarters of a century ago. She and her husband, Juan Domingo Perón, were responsible for the downfall of Argentina, ranked as one of the most prosperous economies in the world during the early part of the 1900s. A chronic underperformer since then, facing constant economic, political, and social crises, this large and important nation has yet to recover. Generations of Argentines have come and gone in the vain hope of seeing their country once again occupy its place among developed nations.

As in *Evita*, the phenomenally successful show, which premiered in London in 1978, *Hugo Chávez The Musical!* mixes autobiographical facts and events with a strong dose of fiction. By embellishing Chávez's already dramatic story, this work avoids the heavy-handed approach of a historical documentary. Most importantly, the musical and dance backdrop allows this remarkable tragic tale to reach a more diversified audience. After all, music is the universal language.

A HYBRID FORMAT
Short Novel and Stage Play Combined

This unique short novel, presented as a stage script for a musical, features QR codes and hyperlinks to diverse music and dance samples. Numerous images throughout the text highlight key figures and events. The format *does not* conform to theater or film script standards, nor is it a "performance-ready" version, as I wrote it for the general reading public rather than industry producers or professionals.

As a hybrid of a novel and stage play, this work combines narrative storytelling and dialogue-driven scenes with music and dance. It harks back to the tradition of zarzuelas and operettas, but with a serious tone and a tragic ending. Unlike most zarzuela and operetta librettos, this book can be read independently, as a standalone novel, without the music.

It is a fictional story, based on real life, where the action unfolds on a stage rather than in the outside world. The musical samples and lyrics add a powerful dimension to the work, creating a unique fusion of three elements: a short novel, theater, and music. It has all the intensity and drama to inspire an extraordinary opera libretto.

ACKNOWLEDGMENTS
My Appreciation to Friends & Family

- Let's start with my two sons, Alvaro and Silvio, both computer engineers who helped me with the musical's technical "moving parts" (i.e., hyperlinks, QR codes, and website). As a bonus, based on their considerable writing skills, they often made suggestions for improvements to the text and taglines. Many thanks from "Pop."

- My brother, an experienced writer also named Silvio, deserves a special mention. He contributed ideas for scenes and characters that I adopted in this work. In fact, we started this as a joint project, outlining and preparing background material together, but later separated because of other commitments. Still, his creative input, which I deeply appreciate, enhanced this book.

- Some time ago, I requested feedback from eight friends and fellow long-distance bicycling buddies about presenting such a controversial topic as a novelized, musical stage play. They had the courtesy to read and make recommendations on a draft, which evolved into this final version. As an outgrowth of that meeting, we formed a permanent group, now numbering fifteen, which has held monthly discussions for the past three years on topics chosen by the rotating host. We aptly named that association the "Scotch & Nerds Club" to reflect its main ingredients: equal parts of a certain beverage plus lots of friendly intellectual BS. To my "beta" nerds, muchas gracias!

THE AUTHOR

Alvaro Gutierrez moved to New York City with his family at age nine, attended boarding schools, and later studied at the University of Pennsylvania and Wharton. He spent over two decades in his native Venezuela before returning to the United States in 2002, where he now resides.

Having lived extensively in both countries, Alvaro's perspective is especially relevant as the influence of Latino culture continues to grow in all areas of American society. When asked, *"What language do you dream in?"* he found it an intriguing question, given his early immersion in English and his later life in Venezuela.

"It depends on the setting and who I'm talking to," he replied. That, he believes, is the true mark of a bilingual mind—when the language of choice emerges unconsciously in that intimate, uncensored world we call dreams.

Early in 1998, Alvaro met and had a drink with Hugo Chávez, then a relatively unknown presidential candidate. That curious encounter inspired this musical, written so many years later. It is a dramatic tale of ambition, betrayal, and damnation—universal themes that transcend time and place.